The Liquorice Tree

Lisa Talbott

Lineage Independent Publishing
Marriottsville, MD
https://lineage-indypub.com

ISBN (paperback): 9781958418048
First published in the United States of America

Publisher: Lineage Independent Publishing, Marriottsville, MD, USA
Maryland Sales and Use Tax Entity: Lineage Independent Publishing, Marriottsville, MD 21104
www.lineage-indypub.com
lineagepublishing@gmail.com

To all the fabulous residents of Bugios, our little Shangri-la in Central Portugal.

Contents

Foreword

It's funny how small the world really is. A chance meeting, either virtually or in person, can change the course of someone's life. For me, a chance encounter with Lisa Talbott's poetry a little over three years ago has blossomed into a friendship and longstanding business relationship as we work together to publish our written works. Because we are on different continents, separated by an ocean and a pandemic, Lisa and I have never met – but I feel as if I have known her forever.

This book, the latest of Lisa's novels, is a shining example of how chance encounters can change people's lives for good or bad. As I was working through the story, editing a little of this and a little of that, I found the story line to be riveting and compelling – as well as *believable*. I felt like I was part of her characters' lives, a fly on the wall, so to speak, observing the events in real time as they unfolded. I could feel a mother's despair and grief; I could envision her teenage daughter growing up to be a savvy young adult; I could feel the confusion of a little boy who had been separated from his family. Just as importantly, I could envision the locations where the story took place. Lisa has truly become a master of her craft and I look forward to working with her for many years into the future.

Michael Paul Hurd

Prologue

"Parr, I love living here in Portugal. Thank you for bringing me on this trip. I still don't understand why my mum didn't want me 'cos I can't remember doing anything bad, but I like my life now…. Do you, Parr? Are you glad we came here?"

Gary was surprised to hear Ethan's declaration. He'd tortured himself endlessly over the years wondering about the effect his decision had had on the boy. He turned towards him, slowly, studying his young face, trying to search into his soul.

"I've regretted it every single day since, Ethan, yet at the same time regretted nothing. Would I do it all over again? I'd most likely say yes and no at the same time, but I can't say I'm sorry because you've been my reason for living. Thank you for that, Son. You have no idea how much that means to me."

Mummy's little soldier had run an errand to the store. A tin of processed peas was all the boy had gone there for. Nathan was a good boy, adored by everyone. It had only just turned five o'clock but indeed the boy was gone.

*   *   *   *   *

It was Nathan's Second Christmas.

"Lickrish Tree," Nathan said.

"Nathan, it's a Christmas Tree, but it has liquorice canes hanging from the branches, see!" Mandy said.

"Kiss wish Tree," Nathan giggled.

"Aww, that's a lovely name, the Kiss Wish Tree… Kim, did you hear him? No, Nathan, it's a CHRISTMAS tree… Say it, Christmas Tree."

"Lickrish Tree"

Mandy and Kim had to laugh as two-year-old Nathan sat chuckling with black around his mouth from sucking on a piece of the black candy. It would forever be a 'Liquorice Tree' in the Bond household.

*   *   *   *   *

Mandy was exhausted. It was Friday afternoon; end of the working week and she was feeling relieved to have the whole glorious weekend ahead. Her handbag slung over her shoulder, she switched off her PC and hurried into the car park, shouting out "have a good weekend" to her colleagues in her eagerness to get inside the car and drive home to her little family.

Kim would have collected her younger brother, Nathan, from his school, hers being nearby. By the time Mandy pulled up outside their three-bedroomed semi-detached house, she knew full well that Kim would be upstairs, lying on her bed with earphones in, talking to her school pals that she'd only just left, minutes ago, on the phone.

It never ceased to amaze Mandy how her daughter and friends found so much more to talk about since leaving school than whilst they were all there together, but then she remembered how she and Diane had done the exact same thing in their teenage years: Diane Stafford, her Newbridge High School pal for the best part of her teenage years and still one of those faithful friends that never failed to remember her birthday, or send Christmas cards. Those were the years when the telephone sat in the hallway, with a cable, and each call a

12

measured cost, and every household bill-payer chastising everyone for any excessive usage.

Young Nathan, on the other hand, would more than likely be sat at the kitchen table doing his colouring in, or in front of the television watching some wildlife programme. He adored animals, every single one. David Attenborough was his hero, and 'when he was old' he claimed he wanted to be just like him.

Mandy was smiling to herself as she drove the short journey to her home, thinking about how different her two children were. The age gap between the two wasn't a problem and had never been. Kim was twelve, going on twenty, whereas Nathan had only recently turned five. And even though they both had the same dad; her two children were like chalk and cheese in every aspect imaginable.

She parked her car in front of the house and hurried inside, eager to join them and hear their stories of their day at school. "Hi honeys, I'm home," she shouted effusively as she threw her handbag and car keys on the hall table by the front door.

Sure enough, Nathan was sitting cross-legged on the carpeted floor, propped up by the settee, watching some documentary about the Australian tree frogs, found mainly in Queensland. He loved their bright green waxy skins and red eyes, their whole being surreal, and nothing like the frogs he found locally. His delighted face at seeing his mother settling next to him and throwing her arm round his shoulder as they both sat on the floor, made her heart swell.

"Fish, chips, and mushy peas for tea tonight okay with you, Sweetie?" she asked as she kissed the top of his head.

It was music to Nathan's ears. Of course it was okay, who didn't love fish, chips, and mushy peas?

"From the chip shop?" he asked, enthusiastically.

Mandy tapped him on the head, "Hellooo, is it someone's birthday that I've forgotten about? Do I have 'lottery winner' tattooed on my forehead? I think not, officer, just your dear old mother's speciality. I'll just pop upstairs to see your sister and then I'll get cracking peeling the potatoes." Nathan smiled at his mother calling herself old. She would never be old in his eyes.

Kim's bedroom door was slightly ajar, and Mandy knocked apprehensively, not wanting to disturb her almost teenage daughter's conversations.

"Hey Mum, don't knock, just come in. Look, I'm talking with Tamsin, she's got a new puppy. Isn't he gorgeous?"

Mandy jumped on the bed next to her daughter, looking at the image of Tamsin on the phone with her beautiful ball of fur. Indeed, he was gorgeous. In fact, that was an understatement, he was adorable!

"Ooh Tamsin, what a beautiful puppy! What breed is it?"

"Hello, Mrs. Bond, he's a Leonberger, nine weeks old. His name's Bryn and my dad got him last night. These dogs are really good at rescuing people from the water. Mum's not too happy at the moment 'cos she didn't want a big dog, but me and Dad did, so anyway, we named him Bryn after my dad's brother that died in a boating accident years ago."

"I think that's a perfect name for him, very befitting and I can't wait to see him in the flesh, or fur! Oh, Tamsin, I love him!"

Kim turned to her mother expectantly, "Mum, can we have one?"

"Kim, I would absolutely love to have one, I adore dogs, but I'm out at work every day. Would you want to leave a little baby like that on its own for hours on end until we all got back home? Besides, Leonbergers are pedigree dogs and cost a fortune. I couldn't afford to buy us one."

Mandy and Kim continued drooling over Tamsin's puppy,

neither feeling it appropriate to talk.

Mandy left Kim to continue her conversation with her friend and ooh and ahh over the beautiful Bryn, to set about preparing the fish and chips she'd promised them, all the time thinking about that most delightful puppy. How would Nathan react to being gifted such a precious animal? It would be a dream come true for him, of course.

As she set about preparing their evening meal, her mind kept going back to Tamsin's puppy, and then thought about all those other hundreds and hundreds of discarded pets that ultimately ended up in places like Battersea Dogs' Home. That once-adored bundle of fun, its appeal suddenly vanished and the poor thing having no idea why its family no longer loved him.

It was tragic, truly. People didn't deserve dogs sometimes. Dogs give all their unconditional love and loyalty to their family. How could anyone simply discard them so easily? It's sickening but happens all too frequently.

The chips were cooking in the chip pan, the pan reserved especially for the purpose. 'Damn,' Mandy thought, as she realised she hadn't got a tin of peas in her cupboard.

"Kim," she shouted upstairs, "can you nip to the shop and get us a tin of peas, please, Louise?" She chuckled at her attempt to humour her daughter.

"I'll go, Mum," chimed in Nathan. What a little treasure he was.

"Take a pound out of my purse, Sweetie, and the change can be your pocket money."

Five minutes later the chips were ready. The fish was already cooked and waiting in the pre-heated oven. The peas would be mashed up and microwaved in seconds. Just waiting for Nathan.

Chapter 2: Nathan

He had a whole pound coin in his hand. His mum had told him he could keep the change. He would ask Mr Newberry if he had enough money left over to buy the new *Planet Earth* magazine he'd seen displayed on the racks of papers, comics, magazines, etc. He had no idea how much it cost but he knew that Mr Newberry would let him put down a part payment if he hadn't enough.

Mr Newberry's shop was literally round the corner from his house, down the jitty and on the left-hand side.

At the bottom of the jitty, he saw a young man standing beside a white campervan with its doors open. The man appeared to be talking on his phone, laughing and bending down to pick up coins off the floor. Nathan spotted a fifty pence coin the man hadn't noticed, and bent down to pick it up.

"Thanks Nathan," the young man said jovially, "that fifty pence will feed my puppy tonight."

Nathan didn't see any puppy, but he instantly recognised the face of a teacher from his school. He'd only been there for about six months when he left after some sort of accident. He seemed to recall his teacher telling the class that Mr. Parr's wife and son had died in a tragic car accident and that he wouldn't be returning to the school. Nathan's mum had cried and hugged both her children upon hearing the sad news, as did many others crowded around the school gates.

"Hey, come over and have a look at him," the man suggested. "Do you like dogs?"

Of course Nathan liked dogs, and of course he'd love to see him; his mother's lessons on not getting into a car with a stranger didn't seem necessary as everyone liked Mr. Parr, besides, he wasn't a stranger, the whole school knew him.

Gary lifted him up onto the step of the campervan and quickly shut the door, then ran round to the front and jumped into the driving seat. He turned his head round to look at the bewildered boy kneeling on the floor, who appeared confused to see no sign of a puppy dog.

"It's ok, Mate, don't worry, I'm not going to hurt you. The puppy isn't actually here, you see, it's somewhere else. He'll be really glad to see you, I've told him all about you. He loves having someone to play with him, but then, don't all puppies love to play?"

Nathan wasn't secure, kneeling on the floor of Gary's campervan, and he was now moving! He hadn't been to Mr Newberry's yet to buy the tin of peas, and his mum would be waiting for them.

He got up and climbed on the seat to look out of the windows and could see Mrs. Armstrong – an elderly neighbour who everyone said was crazy - walking with a frame as if she, too, was going to the shop. Nathan waved at her, but Mrs. Armstrong didn't wave back; perhaps too much of an effort to remove a hand from her frame.

"Mr Parr," Nathan mumbled, "I didn't get the peas. My mum will be cross with me."

"No, she won't be cross with you, Mate. She knows you're with me. Aww, sorry, I should've told you. I already called your mum to ask her if I could take you to see Barney, and she said, 'Nathan will love him', so you see, your mum has given us her permission."

"But she asked me to go to the shop and buy some peas with this pound and I can keep the change. She's making us fish and chips."

"That's right," said Gary, looking backwards from time to

time, to make sure he didn't alarm the boy, "and that's why we're going to stop soon and get some from the chippie. Would you like to get some fish and chips from the chippie?"

Nathan nodded. He was hungry and that very food from a proper chip shop sounded like a real treat.

He felt at odds, though. He didn't know his mum had given Mr Parr permission to take him to see his puppy. So why did she ask him to go to the shop?

They travelled for about fifteen minutes. "Are we nearly there yet?" asked Nathan, straining to look out of the windscreen.

It was beginning to get dusk already and Nathan was struggling to see out of any of the windows. He didn't recognise anything and all he managed to see with any clarity was his own reflection in the campervan windows.

"I need to wee, too."

"Piss on that old towel next to the seat you're sitting on. We can't stop here."

He was mortified! How on earth was he expected to wee on a towel, in a vehicle that was moving?

He whimpered. He was hungry; the promise of fish and

chips had had his tummy rumbling for ages, and now he was told he had to piss on a towel! His mother would be furious if he did that at home.

"Mr Parr, I don't want to wee on your towel. My mum would tell me off if I did that. Can you take me back home now?"

Gary let out an exaggerated sigh. "Nathan, Mate. We've only just begun our exciting trip. Barney's been looking forward to seeing you. Your mum's gonna be really disappointed with you, isn't she? She told me that you will love this adventure. She said to me, 'Gary, look after my boy and show him a good time. Tell him to be good and do as he's told.' So, you want to disappoint your old ma? Is that it? Do you wanna be a big disappointment to her?"

No; of course, Nathan didn't want to be a disappointment to his mum. He was a good boy; he was his mummy's little soldier. She told him all the time, over and over just how much she valued him. He had to brave it out, this time. He decided he would do as Mr Parr and his mother suggested and enjoy the adventure. His little hand curled around the pound coin his mother had given him to buy the tin of peas, he looked at the rampant lion on the flip side of the coin, trying to remember the story his teacher told the class of its significance, something on the lines of bravery, strength, and valour.

He was determined to be the brave little soldier his mother had always proclaimed him to be and tucked his precious coin down his sock. It was going to be a memento of this day.

Chapter 3: Frantic Mandy

The chips were already cooked. The fish was being kept warm in the oven. Kim was still upstairs in her bedroom talking to Tamsin and notching up every reason for getting one of the sibling Leonberger puppies that she knew she had zero chances of persuading her already-financially-stretched mother into agreeing to buy.

Nathan was dawdling and Mandy was surprised as he could usually be relied upon to run to the shop and back in no time. She assumed there must've been a queue, hence his tardiness.

She mashed a pot of tea, buttered bread, laid the table with condiments, crockery, knives, and forks.

"Kim!" she shouted upstairs, "go to Newberry's and see where our Nathan's got to. Everything's ready, I'm about to serve out."

Kim practically fell down the stairs after smelling the aroma of fish and chips escalating upstairs and plonked herself at the table.

"Your brother hasn't brought the peas back. What's taking him so long? Be a love and nip to the shop and hurry him along."

"Mum!" Kim exclaimed, "Why me? He'll be back any minute. Stop possessing."

These new stupid phrases the young generation were using irritated her.

"Kim! He's been gone ages. Please just humour me and go and see what's taking so long. He only took a pound; I can't imagine a darned tin of peas will cost more than that."

Kim huffed and puffed before reluctantly walking out of the front door and made her way to the shop. It was empty, bar Louise, the middle-aged lady behind the counter whom they had joked about asking for a tin of peas, please, Louise.

No, she hadn't seen Nathan. Old Mrs. Armstrong was the last customer she had served, and that alone had been an ordeal after finding she had tried to hide a bottle of whiskey in her trolley! Sometimes they just kept a tab and presented it to her son when he visited.

Kim stood her ground. "He came here for a tin of peas, Louise. Not ten minutes ago. Surely you remember?"

"Sweetheart," she said, patronisingly, "the whole of Hugglescote knows and loves young Nathan, but he has not been here today, or this evening. "

Kim walked out of the shop, looking up and down the jitty she'd just walked down. But he'd gone there, to the shop. Where else would he have gone?

She ran home. "Mum, Louise says he's not been there. He's not in the jitty either, I've looked everywhere."

Mandy looked at the clock on her cooker. She saw the fish batter getting darker inside the oven door. The chips were congealing on the plates. Where on earth was he?

She needed reassurance. She didn't trust her daughter's account of Louise's statement; she needed to go and see for herself. It would take less than two minutes to get to the shop. She was walking swiftly down the jitty, spotted a penny on the cobbled path and bent down to pick it up. 'Find a penny, pick it up, and all day long you'll have good luck'. She smiled as she grasped it in her hand, feeling positive her son would appear any minute.

"No, Love, like I told your daughter, Kim; Nathan hasn't been here today."

"But he must have been. He came to get a tin of peas. You must remember. We only live round the corner. Where else could he have gone?"

Louise was becoming impatient. First the daughter, now the mother! How many times did she need to say she hadn't served her boy? She bit her tongue, "Sorry, can't help you."

Mandy left the shop feeling not just dejected, but angry, hopeful that by the time she returned home he would be there, sat at the table, and all would be just dandy.

But he wasn't sat at the table when she returned, it was just Kim tucking into her food, mopping up the tomato sauce with a slice of bread and butter.

Mandy's appetite had gone. Her mind was racing away, trying to come to some conclusion as to where her boy was. He was five years old. Nathan didn't have a mobile phone, nor was he streetwise. He was young, he was innocent, trusting, and kind. He was her baby, and – she was beginning to consider - now missing!

"999. Please state your emergency."

"Police, please." (She was very tempted to say 'Police, please, Louise'.)

A second later, a female voice spoke to her. "Good evening, Coalville Constabulary, how may I help you?"

"Hello," Mandy's voice quivered, "erm, my little boy hasn't

come back from the shop. He's only five years old. It's not like him."

"How long has been gone?" the lady asked perfunctorily.

Mandy looked at the kitchen clock on the wall, trying to gauge exactly the time Nathan had left the house. She wasn't too sure.

"About twenty minutes, twenty-five."

"It's not really a long time, is it? Name, please."

"Nathan," she answered.

"Your name!"

"Oh, yes of course, sorry. Mandy. Mandy Bond. You see, he'd only gone to the corner shop which is a stone's throw away. He should have been back ages ago. It's not like him. I've been to Newberry's just now to ask about him and they say he hasn't even been there. I'm worried."

"Newberry's, you say. The corner shop, on Forest Road?"

"Yes! But Louise, the lady who works there, tells us he hasn't been there, but he must have done. There is nowhere else he would have gone."

"Have you tried calling him? His friends? Have you gone

looking for him?"

"He's only five!' Mandy was nearly screaming as her voice broke in panic.

She was feeling uncomfortable with the lady's questions, embarrassed at her accusatory assumption of 'bothering' her. Nathan didn't have a mobile phone so she wouldn't have been able to call him. And no, she hadn't called any of his friends because she hadn't thought that he would have gone off without telling her.

Regaining her composure, Mandy continued. "He's five years old, he doesn't have a phone. Please, can you do something? I'm getting really worried about him."

"A missing person is usually taken into consideration a little longer than twenty minutes, Mrs. Bond. If your son hasn't come home in another hour, please feel free to call back. In the meantime, can I suggest you call his friends or go out and have a look for him? In our experience we usually find they come home once they start getting hungry."

Mandy ended the call, feeling useless and confused. That woman on the end of the phone didn't know Nathan like she did. It wasn't in his nature to go off without letting her know where he was going. In fact, it was abysmal that she was fobbed off so flippantly.

She turned to Kim, who had finished eating by now. "Kim, get your coat on, we're going to go out to look for him. Where do you think he would have gone?"

"Aw Mum, do I have to? It's getting dark and Tamsin wants me to call her back. Stop worrying, he'll be back any minute."

Mandy ignored her protests and threw her coat at her, instructing her to put it on and join her. They walked back again to the shop, they walked the length of the jitty in Breach Road looking left to right, right to left.

They started to knock on doors asking if anyone had seen her son. Doors closed with no positive answers being forthcoming. They returned home over an hour later. There was still no sign of Nathan, even though Mandy had left the door open just in case he'd returned while they were out searching.

She was practically hyperventilating by now and dark thoughts were beginning to penetrate her mind at an alarming speed. She was imagining the headlines in the local newspapers and envisioning her son's face on the local news.

She was mentally preparing the words she was going to need to call her ex to confirm to him once again what an unfit mother she was, and then chastising herself for being so melodramatic at the absurdity that such an unheard-of thing could happen in the very neighbourhood she grew up in.

Of course, there was going to be a logical explanation for the young monkey's inexplicable lack of appearance and woe betide him when he did show his face!

She remembered the occasion when she'd been to Sainsbury's with Kim when she was about three years old. Kim didn't want to sit in the shopping trolley seat, insisting on running up the aisles like a wayward child. Mandy was with her mother, and they had both been surprised to bump into Janette, Mandy's cousin, whom neither had set eyes on for almost two years. After they spent the next ten or more minutes reminiscing, Mandy and her mother looked around for Kim. They couldn't find her anywhere in the shop. They spent ages running around, asking the staff to make an announcement over the Tannoy, only to eventually find her in McDonald's next door eating everyone's leftovers! It was humiliating beyond belief, but oh, that feeling of relief when they found her.

She was thinking of all the ways to punish Nathan for giving her such a fright. She'd definitely ground him in the first instance, that was without a doubt! She'd forbid him to watch any of David Attenborough's documentaries for sure. That would teach him a lesson about worrying her in the future!

But that niggle, at the back of her mind... This was Nathan they were talking about. Nathan - not Kim. Her 'little soldier' that had never caused her a moment's doubt in his whole little life. Her pride-and-joy who tells her she doesn't need to wear make-up every day because she always looks beautiful even when she knew she could look like something the cat had dragged in.

Where was he?

Chapter 4: Nathan and Gary

It was dark now and Nathan was fretting, sitting in the back of the campervan. He was angry that Mr Parr hadn't stopped off anywhere to buy some food. He was embarrassed that he hadn't been allowed to get out to go the toilet, like he'd asked. Nothing felt right.

His mum had been expecting him to return from the shop, so why did Mr Parr say it had all been arranged? What had been arranged, and why hadn't his mum told him or even asked him if he wanted to go with someone he barely knew?

"Can you call my mum and let me speak to her? I don't want to be here; I've got to go home."

Gary was peeved, he hadn't quite expected that, indeed he hadn't thought everything through at all!

He sighed dramatically, again, and made a show of making to call on his mobile. He held it against his ear. "Hang on," he said, "it's ringing."

Nathan watched, anxiously, and then Gary put the phone back in his pocket. "No reply," he said. "I'll try again later."

"Try again now. You didn't leave it long enough. Try my mum

again!" Nathan demanded.

"For crying out loud, *Ethan*, what's your damn problem, Kid? You've just seen me try to call her and she's not picking up."

Nathan recoiled at Mr Parr's sharp tone. "It's not Ethan. My name's Nathan."

"Yeah, yes of course it is. Sorry, Nathan, I forgot. It's just that Ethan sounds like Nathan, so I just forgot." He leaned over, smiling, to look at Nathan, trying to reassuring him.

"Oh, Jesus Christ, what was that?" yelled Mr Parr, as a rabbit hopped into the bright beam of his headlights and darted off to the side. Gary swerved to the right in an endeavour to avoid the startled animal and watched as the rabbit hopped away to safety, relieved that he hadn't hit it.

Nerves were getting the better of him as he began to realise the enormity of what he'd done. The last several hours on the road had afforded him the opportunity to think.

With the campervan now set on track and moving slowly, his hands gripping the steering wheel, his heart palpitating, he considered — for a second or two — turning around, dropping the child back at the corner shop. But it was all far too late. The boy would tell his mother. The police would be on his tail. He could go to prison, and he couldn't go through that.

Nobody would understand what he'd been through, his grief, his loss. They would assume he was a pervert, wanting to take the boy for disgusting reasons like was so often the case in child abductions.

But not Gary. He wasn't that kind of man: he was one of the good ones. He'd been a wonderful, doting dad, a loving husband. God had dealt him a bitter blow which he hadn't deserved, and neither had his family. He couldn't dwell on his thoughts or feelings right now. He had to carry on, he had a ferry to catch, and he was still hours away.

He also knew that, by now, the boy's mother would have notified the police that he was missing, and a search party would be out in force, looking for him. It would be on the local television stations, the national television stations, the internet.

"Nate, are you ok? Sorry about the abrupt swerving back there but I couldn't run over the little bunny, could I? Anyway, he hopped safely away so we can get moving more quickly again, and I promise you once we get there, in about another half an hour, we'll get something to eat. I'm starving, I'm sure you must be, too?"

There was a long queue for the ferry at Portsmouth. Cars, vans, campervans, lorries. Everywhere was lit up with the glaring lights. People were mingling outside their vehicles, smoking, laughing, checking tyres, and talking on phones, and Nathan could see it all. He had gone past the feeling of being tired and wanting his bed, his adrenalin was keeping him awake.

The queue started to disperse towards the passport control booths and vehicles began to emerge from different directions. Gary shouted at Nathan to lie down on his seat and close his eyes. The tone of his voice told him he should acquiesce.

"Passport, sir?" the young lady in the booth called. Gary handed over the required documents. She studied them.

"My boy's asleep here," he nodded towards the back. "It's been a long day for him. Do you need me to open the door so that you can see him?"

"No Mrs. Parr with you, sir? This passport is a family one."

"My wife died a few weeks ago. I have the death certificate here," he replied, scrambling through his papers and thrust the death certificate forwards. "Ethan and I are leaving the UK to make a new start, you understand."

The young lady in the tiny kiosk studied the death certificate and the passport and tapped away at her computer.

"I'm sorry for your loss, sir. I hope you and your little boy can find salvation in your new venture. Enjoy your passage to Santander. Make your way to Line C and you will be directed from there, and *Bon Voyage.*"

A flood of relief filled him. So far, so good. Surely it was now just plain sailing?

Chapter 5: Calling the Police

Mandy could hardly speak to the kindly police lady sitting in front of her. Her lips were dry, she kept applying lip balm, then sipping at the glass of the water in her trembling hands. She got up from her seat and moved to the window, anticipating seeing Nathan strolling back to her front door. She sat down again, crossing her arms then her legs. She was agitated and couldn't keep a limb still.

Detective Superintendent Sean Doyle was an exceedingly charismatic man, an expert in such cases like this, her missing son. He'd been in the force for thirty-five years and could tell - normally within seconds of meeting the families - whether anything odd was was apparent. And Mandy had seen far too many videos on the internet to be blinkered to the fact that in cases like this, family members were ultimately, always, the prime suspects.

How often had she lay in bed with her iPad, once her two children were fast asleep, watching all the numerous atrocities played out before her and she, too, would make that easy, carefree, assumption of whodunnit. Is that what the general consensus of opinion would be? That she would be held responsible for her son's disappearance. Her ex certainly would.

DS Doyle sat opposite Mandy who sat aside the young police lady, Paula Duff. Doyle and Duff, Mandy thought. What could they do to bring her baby back home?

"I don't know what else you want me to tell you. I gave him a pound coin to get some bloody peas for our dinner. Oh God, I'm going over and over the same thing. I can't say anymore. Nathan doesn't just go off anywhere without telling me where he's going. I've no doubt loads of other kids do, but he doesn't, he's not like other kids. Why are you continuing to ask all these inane questions when you should be out there looking for him?"

DS Doyle looked down into his folded hands resting on his knees, then looked up as he asked, "Nathan's father? Can you tell me the story? Is he on the scene, have you spoken to him?"

Mandy knew this question was looming. She'd been dreading talking about her ex - and making the call.

"Ugh! He's going to revel in this. He's going to put all the blame on me, again. All this is going to prove to him that I am that unfit mother he's always claiming I am. No, sir! I haven't yet been brave enough to do that. Be my guest and confirm all his accusations. His name's in my phone, here, it's under P for

Pig. His parents had a warped sense of humour naming him James because believe me, Brooke would have been more befitting."

"Mrs. Bond, we can get someone to call on him and explain everything to him. Perhaps it would be better that way. Do you think Nathan could be with his father?"

Mandy wanted to laugh out loud at the obscurity of that scenario! She couldn't remember the last time her once beloved husband had set eyes on either of his children. Six months? More?

"Knock yerself out, mister, and do me the favour. He's not in my phone as Pig for no reason, you understand. The man's a wanker. Pity his dad wasn't! There is no way Nathan would be with him."

Doyle bristled at the vulgar way she'd just described her ex, and in front of her daughter! He hated to hear – especially women – using foul language. He *never* did, and neither did any of his family. His mother had taught him a lesson at a very early age, after he'd recited a little ditty he'd learned: 'I'm a little boy scout, I don't swear. Shit, bugger, arsehole, I don't care.' He was about six or seven years old, and his mother had overheard his prowess. She was that horrified, she'd grabbed him by the scruff of his neck and dragged him indoors where she proceeded to wash his mouth out with soap.

"Do you have a relatively new photograph of Nathan I can see? Also, can you tell me what he was wearing when he left the house to go the shop?"

Mandy took a sharp intake of breath as she realised the depth of the question she'd just been asked. She tried to recall the clothes he had on, and the most recent picture she had of him. It was unimaginable that she was going to have to look through her phone and give the DS one of her treasured pictures. And what was he wearing?

"Uhm, err, well, he had his school trousers on, and his school jumper. They're grey. Oh look, I found this picture of him," she exclaimed whilst scrolling through the photographs on her phone. "This is his first day at school," she managed to smile at the memory of him standing against the front door, chuckling at remembering how proud he felt in his school attire, his rigid stance with his arms firm against his sides, his face tilted upwards. Like a little soldier.

"And there's this one, here, that I took a couple of weeks ago when we were at the park."

The image of him sitting on the grass; his cap at an angle atop his head over his gorgeous little face, his matching mustard-colored jumper, gloves, and boot laces, broke her.

"It's almost 11 o'clock at night! He should have been tucked up in bed hours ago and he's not. Nathan has never, *ever*, given me a moment's worry. I can't just sit here doing nothing but answer your barrage of questions; I'm sorry, Mister Whatever-your-name-is, but I have got to go back out there again and look for him. He *must* be around here. Kim? Kim! Come with me."

When Mandy and Kim walked out of their front door, they were taken aback, seeing a sea of familiar faces of neighbours, school friends, policemen and women milling around solemnly. It was reassuring to her that everyone was coming onboard and making a big show of trying to find her little lad.

As Mandy stood in the glow of her front door, all heads turned towards her and her daughter who stood just behind.

"Please help us to find Nathan." She broke down, turning to Kim for support.

"Why would you let a five-year-old go shopping, alone? What kind of mother would wait until this unearthly hour to notify the police of his disappearance? What have you done with him?" someone shouted in the fray of searchers. The mood in the crowd had suddenly become hostile.

Mandy staggered at the verbal attack hurled at her, and visibly shook. Apparently, it was going to seem obvious to all and sundry that she was to blame, as if she didn't blame herself enough. If only she had insisted Kim go, as she'd asked in the very first place until Nathan had stepped up and volunteered. She should've gone herself, indeed. What diligent mother would allow an innocent boy to do her running? But it was only to the corner shop, for crying out loud! Literally, just around the corner. She'd never wanted to dampen his ardour to grow up and feel he was contributing to the family needs! Kids need to feel appreciated, give them some freedom to evolve and form their personalities. Make them feel important with each little responsibility they're being given.

One of her work colleagues had often told the story of how he, at the age of fourteen, had been given instructions and a bus ticket to get himself to Ireland alone! Was it that it was safer back in those days?

Although the heckle had come from just the one person, Mandy was overcome with shame and anger. How could her own neighbours think, for even a second, she had anything to do with her son's disappearance?

Mandy spoke to the small crowd, "If our own children aren't safe to be within a hundred yards of their homes in this neighbourhood, then – before you start pointing the finger of blame at me – you search your own conscience. You all know me, and you all know my Nathan, and instead of trying to make matters worse it would be much appreciated if you could help us. He'll be frightened. He's five years old. He should be in his bed . . . "

DS Doyle put a comforting arm around her shoulders and led her back inside, leaving the throng of searchers, and in no doubt that it was going to be a long night.

Gary and Nathan left the campervan, following the other passengers, and went to find the cabin they'd been allocated. It was a single berth, Gary had booked a week prior, but felt thankful to see two single beds inside.

"We're going to be travelling across the water on this big boat, Nathan, and it's going to take a long time, so once we've had something to eat, we will sleep in here. Didn't I tell you what an exciting adventure this will be?"

"I haven't brought my toothbrush," Nathan whispered.

"Look, Son, that doesn't matter right now. I'll get one from the shop upstairs, later. I'll get you some more clothes, too, when we get to Spain."

"Spain!?" exclaimed Nathan, "we're going to Spain? I haven't got my swimming trunks either."

Gary stifled a chuckle. "We're driving *through* Spain, then we're going to Portugal. Have you ever been to Portugal, Nathan?"

Nathan shook his head. No, he hadn't been to Portugal, never heard of it, nor had he been to Spain. Some of the boys in his school had been there on holiday and they all said it was lovely and sunny. Nathan had never been anywhere on holiday; his mum could never afford it. He was beginning – slightly – to understand why his mum had given Mr. Parr permission to take him on this trip. He was going on a real adventure, and he was going to have so much to tell Kim and his mum when he got back. He managed to raise a little smile when his tummy rumbled.

"Time for some food, I think," declared Gary, "come on, let's go and see what culinary delights they're serving upstairs."

The ferry was an impressive vessel, huge staircases, brass pillars and gleaming glass screens everywhere; thick, plush red and gold carpets, ornamental statues, music playing from all speakers which served to distract from being on the open seas. *It was like being in a moving hotel,* thought Nathan.

The restaurant was filling up with hungry passengers and both Gary and Nathan knew exactly what they wanted to order. "Two fish and chips, please," and for the first time in hours, Gary smiled, feeling calmer as he watched the delight spread across Nathan's little face.

An hour later, they were both back inside their cabin. Nathan sat on his bunk, his eyes blinking in an endeavour to keep awake.

"It's been a long and exhausting day, Mate, let's hit the sack and get some sleep, hey? The sea's calm, so I guess we'll have a smooth crossing. The last time I made this trip, it was horrendous! People were throwing up all over the place, there were piles of sick everywhere! We got lucky today, don't you think?"

Nathan didn't know what to think. He'd never been on a boat like this one before.

"Did you take someone else on a trip then?" Nathan asked.

Gary nodded, remembering the last time, last year. Ethan was going to have his third birthday in Portugal because Sarah was adamant that he got to know his roots. She wanted to have a photograph of him standing next to his grandfather's graveside. It was the last trip they had together, and it was supposed to be one of many, if fate hadn't decided otherwise.

"Yes, I did, Nathan. And let me tell you, that boy was just the same as you, nervous at first because he had never been away from home, or been aboard a big boat like this, but he was brave, like you, and he loved it. He loved Portugal because it was sunny every day. He had the mountains to climb, the trees to shelter under, the rivers to paddle in. He was trying to learn to speak a little Portuguese, too."

Gary stopped talking. The memories were painful and the words got stuck in his mouth. He hadn't had anyone sit and listen to his stories about his son, his wife, his loss.

He smiled at the expectant young face before him, the one who looked SO much like his Ethan. How could he be doing so wrong when it was all so easy and therapeutic for him?

"And did he?" asked Nathan.

"Did he what?"

"Speak Porchageeze?"

"Portuguese? Ha ha, he did! He picked it up very quickly. You will too, because all your teachers told me how smart you are."

The Atlantic Ocean was being inexplicably kind to all the passengers aboard the huge vessel bound for Santander. There had been no queues in any of the toilets for those having to unwillingly throw up their expensive restaurant food.

Nathan had managed to eat the food Mr. Parr had bought, purely out of hunger. He'd had nothing other than his packed lunch since midday and it had been late evening by the time they did actually sit down to something substantial.

52

He'd been subdued yet overwhelmed by the enormity of everything he was witnessing, trying to understand how the monstrosity of a craft could possibly keep afloat, considering the hundreds of vehicles and people that were embarking. He hoped the 'captain of the ship' was a good 'driver' and wouldn't run into any dolphins or whales.

Afterwards, when he was back at the bunk he was expected to sleep in, a bed - alien to anything he'd ever seen before - in a room devoid of any of his usual home comforts or possessions, no mummy kisses to wish him goodnight as he was being tucked up, sharing the night with a man who assured him it was going to be an exciting adventure, he felt sick. He felt uncomfortable in the expectation he was going to have to sleep in his underwear, wondering why his mother wouldn't have thought to have sent his favourite glow-in-the-dark skeleton pyjamas, his toothbrush, and a change of clothes.

He'd asked his teacher to telephone his mum so he could talk to her, to ask the question why when he remembered the warnings she so often recited about getting into a car with strangers, so why HAD she thought this surprise trip would be good fun? But his mum hadn't picked up the phone and he still had no answers.

He couldn't ever remember Kim going on such a trip; he couldn't remember he or his sister ever spending a night away from their mum before, and this troubled him during his attempt to sleep.

He asked himself why none of the other boys or girls in his school were joining them. Was it a special treat, as Mr Parr had said, or was it more the punishment he felt it was?

The vast construction of the ferry rocked gently, rhythmically, as it made its journey across the waters, but still sleep evaded him. It was impossible to see out of the porthole window as only the moonlight afforded a glimpse of the night sky. He had this gut feeling that something wasn't right and that he'd done something very wrong - enough to make his mother angry and he was desperate to ask Mr. Parr to call her again and let him speak to her. If he had done something wrong, he would apologise and promise not to do it again and his mum would laugh and forgive him of course, but he couldn't think what it was he'd done wrong.

He thought about the pound coin he'd tucked in his sock and wondered if his mum and sister were asleep in their beds or were they - like him - awake and thinking similar thoughts, missing him.

With Nathan eventually asleep in his bunk bed wearing only his underpants, his little cheeks glowing a healthy pink, Gary leaned over to him and planted a kiss on his forehead. He so much wanted to envelope him in a big hug, smell him, hold his hand and count his breathing, but now wasn't the time for physical contact. He needed to gain the boy's trust: he hoped he could achieve it.

Once they arrived in Santander, Gary knew it would take approximately six to seven hours to drive over to Portugal, providing everything was in their favour and there were no unforeseen mishaps, or that snow hadn't blocked the route over the Estrela mountains. He felt confident that Nathan hadn't been seen on any CCTV anywhere and doubted there would have been any in the canteen on the ferry. He was also sure that once they reached Portugal, he would feel less anxious.

Nathan looked so much like Ethan it was uncanny. He'd noticed that when he was working at the school. They could easily have been considered brothers. Twins, almost! And ironically, they had similar names. It had been amusing while he was working there, seeing another little boy who looked the same. He'd joked with Sarah about their obvious similarities and how the two would have such fun with the teachers when Ethan joined upon reaching eligibility. He assumed they would become instant buddies, each having a doppelgänger to play with in the school playground.

The ferry pulled into Santander in the very early hours of Sunday morning. It was overcast and damp. Tired passengers sat in their vehicles, eagerly waiting to disembark, in long queues.

Gary hadn't bothered to shower or shave and as Nathan had been fast asleep in his bunk, he decided not to bother waking him until the last moment. Now they both sat in the front seats of Gary's campervan, awaiting their turn to follow the stream of revving vehicles heading into Spain.

He manoeuvred his gear stick into first, moving slowly behind the gleaming black Mercedes that was indicating to go right. Gary indicated to go left and switched up to second gear; the morning Spanish sun trying to force itself through the grey clouds to shine a welcome to the newcomers.

"Nearly there now, Mate, just a few more miles to go and you will see the most amazing things you could only imagine. Ethan, you... sorry... Nathan, you will feel like you've come home. It's all gonna start here. Barney is going to love you."

Chapter 7: Bugios

It was December 1st, just three more weeks to go until Christmas. It was going to be Gary's first as a widower; without Sarah, his beloved wife; and Ethan, his gorgeous boy. It didn't seem possible. This time last year they were busy making plans for the festive season.

He acknowledged that it was also going to be Nathan's mum's first Christmas without her boy; Kim's without her brother. This Christmas, Nathan wouldn't have the excitement of sending his letter to Santa Claus up the chimney because he wasn't going to be at home with his mum and sister, he was going to be in Portugal, with Mr. Parr.

But Nathan hadn't even contemplated it being December and nearly Christmas because the sun shone brightly every day and it was still surprisingly warm.

He'd been in Portugal for almost two months now and his face shone with health. He and Barney had bonded like superglue and had become inseparable, with Barns (as he was now known) sleeping on his bed and following his every move. He couldn't even bathe or go to the toilet without the dog at his heels.

Gary had been cutting down an enormous old bay tree from the bottom meadow. He hated the damned trees with a passion as they always seemed to sprout shoots everywhere! The leaves fell and covered every pathway. A million pounds worth if he could have been bothered to bag some and sell them.

The burning curfew had been lifted so it gave him the opportunity to set fire to a huge number of branches, the aroma of the bay leaves permeating the air as they crackled in the flames. He sawed the trunk and outer branches, stockpiled it in readiness for the oncoming cold weeks.

Sarah would've been in her element. She adored coming to Portugal; it was in her veins. She was always the one who undertook stacking up the wood for their log burner. She'd delight in spending hours foraging for the pinecones, coming back with bags full. She'd place a couple, intermingled with last year's dried out and chopped up fig tree branches, before igniting it with a match. "This is the life," she'd chuckle as she sat back next to Gary on the floor, watching the flames dance and warm the whole house. And it was 'the life'. It *WAS*!

How every single thing had changed in such a short time. He'd never forget 'that day'. The one when he observed the police car drive up to the school gates and wondered what on Earth brought the police to the school. Oh, he found out soon enough...

He tried to push the thoughts from his memory, he needed to be clear headed to convince everybody and himself that Nathan was Ethan, even to the point of suggesting he drop the use of Mr. and just call him 'Parr.' Rather cunning, he concluded, because to all intents and purposes the boy was calling his 'father' Pa. How sweet. None of the locals in the village had the slightest inclination that he wasn't, even though they all sympathised effusively upon learning his story of how Sarah had lost her life in the car accident but were overjoyed at having young 'Ethan' back in Bugios, bringing new life into the old 'ghost town' of a place.

Many a morning Gary would find a couple of cabbages beside his front door, a bucket of potatoes, a dozen fresh eggs. It was typical of his wonderful Portuguese neighbours, and he would reciprocate by gifting them a sack of oranges or tangerines from his bountiful fruit trees.

He was so pleased with himself for deciding to get the puppy. Isabel's German Shepherd had given birth to three delightful bundles of mischief, two *cadelas* (females) and one *macho* (male) eight weeks prior to the pair of them arriving. The timing couldn't have been more perfect, and Isabel had agreed to keep Barney for two more weeks until he was ready to leave his mum.

At first, Nathan was apprehensive about being given the puppy, recalling his mother telling Kim they couldn't afford a dog, how it would chew anything and everything, and how many were in kennels or dog pounds waiting for their forever home, but Gary went to great lengths to explain - again - that this was a new life for him now, too, and Barney would need his love and support to help him get over the loss of *his* mother and sisters.

That indeed struck a chord. He felt an overwhelming sense of duty to love and care for this little pup, and so the boy decided it was time to toughen up.

*   *   *   *   *

Mandy did not want to deck the house with Christmas trimmings. She didn't want to buy a 'Liquorice Tree' as Nathan had always called Christmas trees, write out cards to wish everyone a happy Christmas because she didn't want anyone to be happy when she was slowly dying.

It was eight weeks now. Eight whole agonising and ugly weeks since she'd heard her darling boy's childish voice, saw his beautiful happy smile, felt his soft skin, or smelled his sweet, delicious scent. She had never been a religious person until now when her soul had been turned over by the big man Himself and she had prayed a hundred times a day. She had begged God to forgive every wrong she'd ever done if he would at least keep him safe!

She hadn't changed the sheets on his bed. She hadn't washed his glow-in-the-dark 'skeleton-themed' pyjamas. She left his bedroom door ajar all the time, hoping, praying, this would be the night she'd receive the telephone call to say he had been found and was coming home.

She had gone over and over THAT night, wondering if there was anything she'd missed. Had Nathan ever mentioned anyone hanging around, trying to talk to him? No, there was nothing she could recall.

She'd exhausted herself night after night watching documentaries about missing children, reading biographies of parents who were in the same position as herself. Some of the abducted children were found years later, others not.

She wondered how those other mums and dads managed

to get out of bed every morning and live through another day. She recalled hearing the news of that young teacher at Nathan's school when he'd lost his wife and son in a car accident, how she'd cried and hugged her children. That poor man, whatever his name was.

It was the 'not knowing' scenario. At least that schoolteacher knew what had happened to his family, he was allowed to grieve, and she knew he would be able to, someday, come to terms with his loss and build a new life. But for Mandy she could not forsee that opportunity.

But now the guilt began to kick in because Kim was still a child and she knew she should make an effort for Christmas for her! How she would love 'the pig' to suggest he have Kim to stay with him over the Christmas holiday so that she could wallow alone without having to force herself to buy presents and feign enthusiasm on Christmas morning, to watch her open something bought out of duty rather than love.

Her Christmas box was up in the attic. No. She couldn't do it. It would be just far too painful. She knew exactly what was in that box and fetching it out of the attic would be like a stab in the heart. How was she going to get through the next few weeks?

It was a quarter past four as Kim waltzed through the front door. She kicked off her fake Ugg boots and slung her coat on the floor at the side of her school bag. Mandy hadn't the energy to reprimand her and tell her, for the umpteenth time, to hang them on the coat hooks that are placed there for that very reason!

"Tamsin says her mum says she's going to get rid of the dog. It's knocked over their Christmas tree and smashed all the baubles she just bought. Tamsin's really mad at her mum cos she loves the dog. Tamsin says it's not fair cos he didn't know, he's only a puppy. Tamsin says . . ."

Mandy interrupted, "No, it's not fair, Kim. You're right, nothing IS fair. *Life* isn't fair! Tamsin is right too; her mother isn't being fair because surely she knew that a puppy that big is going to be a lot of hard work. Is she stupid or what? It isn't fair on our poor Nathan not being able to be here for Christmas either, how would Tamsin's mum cope if one of her kids wasn't able to be sitting round the bloody 'liquorice tree' and enjoying her stupidly expensive baubles, like us, hey? *SHE* is not being bloody fair! That dog didn't choose to go and live with them, *THEY* decided his poor fate. What on Earth is wrong with some people, Kim? They've only just got the poor thing and now, just because it broke a few replaceable knick-knacks, she's throwing in the towel? Well, it just shows what an unfit mother Tamsin has. What a heartless, uncaring, materialistic bitch!"

"Wow, Mum!" Kim was somewhat taken aback at the vitriol spewed from her mother's lips. "You don't even know Tamsin's mum."

"I know enough, Kim. And you have just confirmed all I need to know about her. Love isn't conditional, Sweetheart. You don't give up on love just because some things don't always turn out the way you expect it to."

"You and Dad did."

Mandy took a sharp intake of breath. Her daughter's statement was a body blow.

"Kim. I wasn't the one who stopped being 'in love' with your dad. Good grief, we made you and Nathan. It was your dad who stopped being in love with me! And I'm not about to badmouth your father now because I'm too fragile to go down this road. I'm going to have to get my bottom into gear to prepare some kind of Christmas for you when it's the last thing I want to do because I can't stop wondering what's happened to your brother. I can't bear to think of where he is, who he's with, what they are doing to him or why they took him. I can't bear the thought of waking each morning and realising he isn't here with us, Kim. I'm the one here for you and Nathan, always have been, always will be. I love the bones of you two and I loved your dad, I did not give up on *HIM*! One day when you're old enough to know the true meaning of love, Kim, you might just get an inkling of what the word really means."

Kim stood rigid, hardly daring to move. Her mother's verbal outburst had saddened her.

"I'm sorry Mum, I didn't mean it like that. We know you love us, and we're glad it's just us three. I miss Nathan too, you know. The best thing – in fact the only thing - that I could wish for Christmas is to have him back home. You always made our Christmases perfect; it will be again, you'll see."

Mandy's head dropped as she sobbed. She felt wretched for raising her voice and causing her daughter to feel on tenterhooks; she hadn't deserved it. She had dismissed even thinking about what she was having to go through, at school, the questions, the discussions out of her earshot.

"So, Tamsin's destructive puppy. Wotsisname. Are they really going to get rid of him?" Mandy turned to look at Kim, wiping her eyes on the back of her sleeve, waiting for an answer.

"Tamsin thinks so. She says her mum wants to go away for Christmas now, somewhere warm. She took all the trimmings off the tree and dumped everything in the dustbin, all the broken baubles." Kim started to laugh, nervously, "I wish I could have seen it, Mum. You know, Bryn racing round their Christmas tree thinking it was a huge game. Ha ha ha. Poor thing, he wasn't to know, was he? He's just a puppy."

Kim joined Mandy sitting at the kitchen table, laughing at the thought of Tamsin's mum screaming blue murder at the mischievous pup as he was hell bent in ruining her festive artistry.

It was a beautiful moment, the two of them finding something to laugh about at the expense of someone else's misfortune for a change. It felt good.

Chapter 8: Kim- aged 12 (*in her own words*)

My brother has been missing for weeks now. I ought to remember the actual date; have it indelibly etched into my memory bank, but I don't. I'm sure mum has, in fact I KNOW she has as her every conversation revolves around 'before Nathan got lost', or 'the day after Nathan went missing'. Everything that happens now or happened way back, revolves around the timeframe of my brother's disappearance.

My schoolteacher, Mrs. Green, says that that is normal, it's like part of the grieving process because it is like a bereavement but without the actual knowledge and proof of them being dead. I can't even begin to contemplate Nathan being dead.

As I say, it's been weeks, and the police haven't been able to come up with a single clue. Which is strange because no one can simply disappear off the face of the earth, can they? Somebody must know something, saw something.

My brother is a nice kid, a bit crazy, but I like him. He's a good boy, not like some of my friends' brothers or some of the boys at school who are really horrible. Nathan isn't horrible, he's . . . well, he's Nathan.

And I haven't told Mum this, but I feel dreadfully guilty about the whole thing because she'd asked *me* to go to the shop and I whinged cos I was talking to my friend, Tamsin, on the phone. She'd just had a new puppy, Bryn. He's a Leonberger and just the most gorgeous thing ever; and then goody-goody Nathan chimed in offering to go instead.

If I hadn't been insistent on talking with Tamsin and gone to Newberry's as mum asked, Nathan wouldn't be missing. Mum wouldn't be crying all the time; Dad wouldn't be phoning her, shouting at her and making her even more depressed. She'd be looking forward to Christmas, as we did every December.

I'd have clean clothes to wear, too, because Mum would have done the washing and ironing as she always did. She hasn't put the washing machine on for weeks now, nor even changed my bed sheets. I don't really care about my bed sheets, but my school shirts got a bit smelly and I had to start washing them, and my underwear, in the bathroom sink. I don't want to say anything about this because I don't want her to shout at me for bothering her about such trivial things.

They're not trivial things to me, though. You see, one of the girls in my class at school has started her periods and she told us all that we would be getting ours too, soon! I need to talk to

Mum about it, but I don't want to add another thing for her to worry about.

I don't have any aunties to talk to about these matters, so I listened to Rebecca, the girl who's just started her periods; we all did. Rebecca's mum explained everything that was happening to her, and why. She bought her some tampons as she said they were better than the alternatives, but she didn't tell her what the alternatives were, so Rebecca showed us a tampon and what it was for and where it went!

I'm nearly thirteen years old and had no idea that I had a place on my body where I was supposed to stick a tampon into! It was frightening, I tell you!

Anyway, at least I now know and when the inevitable does happen I will be somewhat ready.

Being prepared for such a monumental thing to happen in one's life, is a good thing, yes? But we weren't, nor could ever be, prepared for what happened to our little family when Nathan didn't come home that night. A simple little errand like going to the shop down the road; the shop we've been going to every day.

The internet and television coverage has been embarrassing

with their never-ending use of the fact that he'd gone to get a tin of peas. It feels as if they're making fun. But it's not funny at all.

They've put Nathan's picture up everywhere. The one with him wearing his cap and blue denim coat. It's a lovely picture. We were at Bradgate Park that day, just a week before. Before Nathan went missing. I think that photograph will always remind me of that day we went to Bradgate Park.

Nathan is a big, big fan of David Attenborough. He has like a million DVDs and goodness knows how many books of his. He can't read all the big words in some of the books, but it doesn't matter to Nathan, the man is his super-hero.

According to my little brother, David Attenborough grew up in Leicestershire, where we live, so he feels he has this affinity with him. Apparently - again according to my brother - David Attenborough's interest was ignited after finding a fossilised rock just a couple of miles away in Whitwick, in a wooded area close to where we live!

You should see Nathan's bedroom, it's full of bizarre things. He has a display cabinet of creepy crawlies (dead ones, of course! Mum wouldn't let him bring live ones indoors). He has a huge map of the world on his wall with little coloured pins stuck in every country that David Attenborough has visited.

He once found the skeleton of a baby rabbit and he has all the bones in a shoe box that he keeps in his underwear drawer. I kid you not, if you didn't know my little brother you would think he was a nutcase, but Nathan isn't a nutcase. Like I said, he's a cool brother.

So, anyway. I kinda understand that Mum doesn't feel enthusiastic about Christmas because she's sad and worried about Nathan, but I want her to stop being sad, until at least Christmas is over. I desperately want some proper Ugg boots but I daren't tell her that because then she'd feel she has to go out, to the shopping centre, and find some for me.

Mum hasn't been shopping since before *that* day. Not for a big shop, like she used to. For the first couple of weeks she didn't cook anything, not a thing; the neighbours brought food round, every day. We just lived on whatever food was left on our doorstep, basically. Not that Mum or I could actually face a lot of food. We couldn't think about putting anything in our mouths because our stomachs felt tight with worry, if you know what I mean. Mum was constantly flying up the stairs to the bathroom to be sick. The smell of coffee or cooked food would trigger her off.

And when Mum is feeling like this, it makes me feel like I shouldn't be eating anything, either. But while she doesn't ever feel hungry, I do, but I don't know how to tell her that.

We have a pantry in our house which is never not full of stuff that Mum buys when certain things are either reduced or on special offer, so there are always at least six tins of tuna, baked beans, bags of pasta, tinned tomatoes, jars of beetroot and pickles. The freezer is bursting at the seams with fish fingers, ice cream, garlic breads, and bags of frozen vegetables, which is ironic when you consider Nathan had gone to the shop to get a tin of peas when there was a bag of frozen ones in the freezer. She could have taken some out of the bag and put them in the microwave which would have taken a lot less time . . . blah blah blah.

Anyway, that's hindsight, isn't it? I bet Mum thinks the same thing if she dared admit it.

It was Christmas Eve afternoon: still glorious and sunny and such a contrast to what Gary knew the weather would be like, back in Blighty. Outside, the sun shone brightly, warming the white plastic chairs he'd found aside one of the skips. Possibly discarded by a neighbour as they looked, to all intents and purposes, beyond salvageable. He hadn't got any seating facilities so he concluded anything was better that nothing. He set to with a sharp knife, scraping the goodness-knows-how-many-years of grime off the outer surfaces of all four chairs, bringing them back to a practically brand-new shine!

Being busy kept him from his ever-invasive dark thoughts. Every day heightened his anxiety and guilt, his grief. He was trying his best to be a good dad, but Nathan wasn't Ethan, try as he may to convince himself and others.

What would Sarah have thought about what he'd done? As a mother she would never have condoned his impulsive and inhumane act. That was beyond discussion. And it would have been for Gary, too, once upon a time. Sarah wasn't here though, to chastise or comfort him. She wasn't by his side to advise, agree or disagree. She was gone, and so was his adored Ethan.

Gary was still bitterly angry with her; she had been the one driving the damned car. She was the one who was supposed to protect their boy, like he always did. How could she have been so careless? It was her fault he was in this predicament now; she is to blame for him taking someone else's son to try to take away the excruciating pain of being without his reason to live.

Nathan was never going to replace Ethan, ever. He didn't smell like Ethan; he didn't talk or laugh like Ethan. He never would, either. But Nathan has taken Ethan's place now, he IS Ethan and he will grow to love him the same... he has to!

The church in Santo Andre das Tojeiras was bedecked with lights proclaiming *'Boas festas'*, life-like nativity scenes, the bonfire waiting to be lit after midnight mass. Neighbours from the surrounding villages would come flocking for the occasion, religious to a fault. Gary had decided he and Ethan would attend, and offered to drive Isabel and Albertina, two widows from Bugios who never wore anything but their traditional black mourning clothes even though their husbands had been dead for over twenty years.

He felt duty-bound to Sarah and her forefathers to attend the vigil; he and Ethan would light candles for their loved ones, along with the others.

The too-modern church in Santo Andre das Tojeiras held none of the charm and warmth of the old churches in Leicestershire, and Ethan quickly fell asleep on Gary's lap. He wished he'd thought to bring a blanket or cushion, remembering the last time he'd been in the church for Antonio's funeral (one of Bugios' old-timers). The Portuguese Catholic services were notoriously longer than Church of England services and were infinitely more mundane because it was - naturally - all recited in Portuguese.

It was way past Ethan's usual bedtime and as Gary tried to move him into a more comfortable position, he woke up. He looked around startled, bewildered at his surroundings, confused to see so many unfamiliar faces and he panicked!

"Parr! Parr, where's Mummy? Parr, I want to go home now."

There was a deathly hush amongst the congregation as all eyes of the elderly community turned their attention to see which of the few youngsters in the church had dared to interrupt the service. Gary's heart began to thump heavily in his chest as he feebly tried to pacify the child. This had not been anticipated, and he was affeared. Ethan started to cry a little louder; his bravery had been shot to pieces and he wanted the comfort and reassurance of his mother.

"I want to go home, Parr. I want my mum."

The spectators were quick to comprehend the boy's distress. After all, the mite had only recently lost his mother in that awful car accident. Whilst none could understand his English words, they all knew the English for 'mum', and 'Pa' for dad! Their sympathetic hearts went out to the new English family, who were trying to integrate into their own close-knit community.

Gary picked up the tearful Ethan in his big arms and rushed out of the church, apologising to Isabel and Albertina in as many Portuguese words as he could muster to explain that he would need to take Ethan home and hoped another neighbour would be kind enough to transport the two of them back to the village. They would forfeit the fun of gathering around the warm bonfire: he had a son to father. They had Barns to feed and keep company; the pup hadn't been left to his own devices for more than thirty minutes before. Gary needed to reassure and settle Ethan in any way he could. It wasn't going to be easy.

Gary cruised the campervan into his driveway, Ethan fast asleep on the passenger seat. The security light came on immediately and flooded the area in an unnatural fluorescent blue, cheating the stars above for their chance to shine on this

Christmas Eve. He turned off the ignition and stared at the sleeping form next to him and was instantly distracted by a scratching and whining sound at his door; it was Barns.

Five minutes later, young Ethan was placed in his single hand-made from wooden pallets bed, fully clothed, with his devoted pup licking his face, depositing smidgeons of jelly from the tin of dog food he just devoured in a millisecond, then all fell silent. Gary stood in the doorway surveying the sight, tormented by his conscience but calmed by the thought of the approaching morning.

The midnight bells were going to herald a brand-new day and he had come through so much. They both had. He knew he had to knuckle down and create a true, positive, structure to their existence here in Portugal. He was under no illusion as to the obstacles and dilemmas he was going to face; they were both going to face, together.

Even before the night would become more than a fleeting memory, Gary and Ethan realized – in sheer disbelief – that they had been lovingly absorbed into their community on the morning they awoke on 25 December. Neither would ever forget the overwhelming generosity and hospitality of their neighbours, discovering an unbelievable amount of goodwill left at their threshold.

Someone had decorated a branch of the huge bay tree Gary had cut down and it now resembled a Christmas tree. They'd stuck it in a bucket and sprayed it with white paint to look like snow. They'd then interwoven a string of battery-powered lights around each arm, hung bright baubles and silver tinsel. They'd left gift-wrapped parcels underneath for Ethan. There was a basket of eggs, a cabbage, a *bolo* (*cake*), a home-made loaf that was still warm and wrapped in a tea towel. A jar of olives, a bottle of olive oil, a huge bone for Barns, a case of beers, and a traditional figurine of the Madonna.

Gary was humbled. He felt he didn't deserve this extravagant show of kindness from these unsuspecting people. *"If only they knew,"* he thought. But he also knew that there was no possibility they should ever know the real truth about him, and Ethan did deserve all their compassion, every inch of it. These people were doing it for *his* Ethan, too. This was their way of reaching out and helping their fellow neighbour.

His passport to Bugios had been stamped with approval from its twenty-four inhabitants. Now he and Ethan were established as part of the village community. He couldn't, wouldn't, disappointment them.

It was with the greatest reluctance that Mandy decided to get the Christmas decorations out and make some kind of effort for the two of them. It was the last thing she wanted to do but it would not have been fair to Kim. She remembered an uncle of hers, who was long gone now, telling her that his own mother never celebrated another Christmas after one of her children died as a toddler. He was but a boy himself and didn't understand why everyone in his school had presents in a stocking from Santa Claus, gift-wrapped boxes under a brightly adorned tree, a huge Christmas dinner with silver trinkets hidden in the Christmas pudding, because he and his family didn't, after the accident. Mandy recalled thinking how sad that must have been for her uncle and his remaining siblings, as if they hadn't mattered to their mother, anymore.

Or was it just a cop out for her, to garner the sympathy vote from all and sundry hereinafter and preclude her from the obvious toil Christmas entailed? Did her uncle's mother associate every Christmas as a time for grieving and pity? Mandy would not allow herself to sink into the same pothole. Kim deserved better than that.

She would endeavour to keep the magic alive for as long as she was mentally and physically able and that meant buying Nathan the presents she would have done as if he was still at home, the things she knew he would write on his list to Santa Claus. They would remain in his bedroom for however long it took until he was home again, because she had no doubt he *would* be home again.

She would order those stupidly expensive Ugg boots that Kim wanted, on-line, because that's what all good mothers do, fulfil their wishes. Why, oh why, had she not gotten someone to fulfil her only wish?

Kim *would* get to wake on Christmas morning with a bulging stocking at the foot of her bed, filled with moisturisers, make-up, hair straighteners; the typically teenage girly wants, stuffed inside an old pair of her tights, before coming downstairs to find an array of lovingly decorated boxes under the tree.

The main surprise present, though, was just that. A surprise. Mandy had deliberated considerably before throwing all caution to the wind. God bless her best friend in the whole wide world - her boss - Mac McNulty, for offering to keep Bryn for a couple of nights.

Mandy couldn't stand the thought of Tamsin's puppy being

unwanted anymore by his family. So what if he broke a few Christmas ornaments and ran riot in their pristine detached with double garage and half an acre of coiffured lawns? Didn't they take that into consideration before splashing out over a grand for a dog? Or was he just supposed to be a status symbol?

The novelty can wear off pretty quickly when you have a young dog intent on destroying everything you hold dear, like a cream leather Italian hand-stitched settee and original Calvin Klein underpants! She couldn't afford more than £300 but Tamsin's mum was happy to let him go to someone she knew and felt patronisingly gracious to almost 'give him away' to the Bonds, bearing in mind their very unfortunate circumstances.

And so good old Mac kindly offered to keep the pup a couple of days until Christmas morning when he would turn up at Mandy's front door with the infamous Bryn.

He was a divine boss. He was a great person, and fortunately a dog lover. He had been totally understanding with Mandy's situation, never pressurising her to return to work until she felt ready. What other boss would do that?

In fact, everyone at her workplace had been outstanding. They'd all rallied round in unison, searching the local terrain, posting 'missing' posters in all the supermarkets, parks, gymnasiums, Facebook, train, and bus stations. They'd diffused negative comments about her being an unfit mother allowing a minor to go shopping unsupervised. They'd organised a whip-round to collect money for a turkey and Christmas cake for her and Kim. It was embarrassing for Mandy, but at the same time, very humbling.

When Kim woke at 7.30 a.m., she hardly dared look to the foot of her bed. She had helped her mother 'trim up' and open some cards they'd received in the post, guiltily remembering her mother hadn't sent any, and noticed a couple of lavishly decorated boxes under the tree, hoping the contents were real, for her, and not just for decoration; and to her joy she found 'He had been'!

She was overwhelmed that her mother had motivated herself to participate when she hadn't even noticed. It wasn't until she joined her mother downstairs that she noticed the gift tags on the parcels under the tree: three for her, three for Nathan, that her heart began to race.

"Open just that big one, Kim, for now. There are two smaller ones that I'd like you to open later on, but after breakfast."

Mandy was sitting cross-legged on the floor, the settee supporting her back, a cup of coffee in both hands, she'd been up since five a.m. Kim put her stocking gifts beside her as she took the largest parcel and tentatively peeled back the cellotape trying not to tear the paper too badly so that her mother wouldn't be able to reuse it another time.

She jumped back and gasped when she noticed the Ugg trademark on the box and decided the wrapping paper would have to end up in the bin as she tore it off in eagerness to get to her much-wanted boots.

Kim was so excited. They fit perfectly and she was going to keep them on all day long, no matter she was in her pyjamas.

"Mum!" she cried, "I love them. Thank you so much, thank you, thank you!" She flung her arms around her mother's neck, and for the next few seconds, they sat there together in contemplative silence, just hugging.

Mandy broke away. "You can open your other two presents later. We'll have some breakfast and I'll get another coffee." She sat for another few seconds staring forlornly at the three gifts waiting for Nathan.

Her reverie was broken by a knock at the door. She jumped slightly. Surely it wasn't Mac at this time in the morning, he said he wouldn't be over until around ten thirty. She was still in her dressing gown, the one that was in dire need of a wash and was beginning to smell a little fusty.

Kim volunteered to see who it was and was practically bowled over by a very young and boisterous Leonberger, a sheepish looking Mac behind, trying earnestly to hold on to his lead: and if Mandy considered she had the weight of the whole world on her shoulders, she would come to realise she would have more.

"I'm sorry to be so early Mandy, but he was driving the missus bonkers while she's trying to get breakfast sorted for all the grand-kiddies. He's already helped himself to half a pound of bacon from the frying pan as well as getting himself completely tangled up in the Christmas tree lights. Last night, he managed to chase the neighbour's cat that pops round to ours every day and the poor thing spent the next hour on the garage roof, frightened to death to come down. I hope you know what you're taking on here. I mean, don't misunderstand me, he's a lovely chap, but he's got tons of energy."

Mandy was half listening to Mac whilst at the same time watching Kim who was being licked to death and pounced upon by this beautiful bundle of white, black, and tan fur, wondering why her friend's dog was in her living room on

Christmas morning.

Mac bid his Christmas wishes and farewells before departing, leaving Mandy and Kim to stare in amazement and wonder how they were going to cope.

Chapter 11: Bryn

Miraculously, Bryn settled down not long after Mac left. It was almost, Mandy thought, that the dog had been dying to get to them!

"You may as well open your other presents now, Kim. Let's get everything done and then we can start to get acquainted with our new family member."

There was a new, blue collar and lead and a dog blanket that Mandy insisted he would be sleeping on in the kitchen. Kim wrapped it around his shoulders as his big eyes studied her face. He licked her face as he lifted his right paw.

"Oh Mum, look! He just gave me his paw."

Mandy gently stroked his forehead and ears, and then he turned towards her and offered her his paw, too. They both laughed.

"Isn't he the most beautiful puppy you've ever seen, Mum?" Kim asked. Mandy nodded, smiling, imagining Nathan's delight too, had he been there.

"I'm so glad you got him for us. Nathan's going to love him when he sees him. Can we take him out for a walk this morning?"

An hour later, even before the breakfast dishes had been packed away, the young Bryn was on his new Christmas lead and yearning to get outside and go for a walk.

It was only a few yards up Forest Road to the vast fields where Bryn would soon know to be his world. He would meet other dogs and their owners; he would be taught not to pull on his lead. There would be a million new smells to enjoy, balls to run after and sticks to fetch.

Dogs have an uncanny perception to humans' problems and Bryn was no exception. After all the horror stories from 'Tamsin's mum' and Mac, and their earlier first few minutes' introduction, Bryn was weirdly calm. After returning from their morning walk, he turned straight into their gate as if he'd turned there umpteen times previously. He didn't bolt through the door, like they expected; he merely trotted through and plonked himself right on the pale grey hearth rug in front of the fireplace. Within minutes he was fast asleep, stretched out as if thoroughly exhausted.

"He is the best Christmas present ever, Mum," Kim told her mother. "Thank you so much. I can't believe you went and got him. I love him already. Do you, Mum? Do you love him?"

"Sweetheart, how could anyone not love him? Apart from Tamsin's mum, hey?" she chuckled. "I've always loved Leonbergers. Did you know that they originated in Germany but practically died out decades ago? I remember reading about an English soldier during one of the wars, can't remember which one now, either the first or second; anyway, he came across a man who owned one and it was really thin. The man could barely afford to feed himself, let alone a big dog like this breed," she said nodding to the sleeping pup, "so he offered to buy it from the man, but the only thing the soldier had to offer in exchange was a bar of soap. The owner agreed to the swap and the soldier eventually brought it back to England after the war ended and began to breed them. They're renowned for their placid temperament, good with children too. And yes, totally beautiful."

Bryn, as if hearing about the history of his lineage, gave a big sigh and wagged his tail.

Meanwhile, back in Portugal, Gary, Barns, and Ethan were walking by the river at Taberna Seca. Gary had put a leg of wild boar in the oven for dinner. It was Christmas Eve roadkill. Driving back from the church in the pitch black, he spotted a whole family of wild boar in his headlights and braked hard to avoid hitting it, stalling his campervan, but it had been too late as one of the piglets altered its course of direction and the next thing Gary knew was the feel of running over a bump. Of all the nights for something this dreadful to happen.

He sat there momentarily, not wanting to get out of his driver's seat to confront what he knew he was going to find. He felt like a murderer on this Christmas Eve and thanked the Almighty that Ethan was asleep and hadn't witnessed it. He picked up the small, bloodied animal and felt its warmth, hoping it was actually dead and not wracked in pain.

He knew he would have to skin and butcher it before Ethan woke in the morning and as he contemplated having to do the task, he cried. And he cried all the way back home, not only for the piglet, but for every misdemeanour he had done/was doing.

Six foot two James Bond was thirty-five and still trying to live the playboy life. He was exactly the proverbial 'Jack-the-lad' waste-of-space his ex-wife described him as. Doyle ascertained that Mandy was right in her assessment of him, not minutes of being in his company.

When he'd knocked on Bond's door at just before midnight on the night of Nathan's disappearance, he'd already categorised the man.

Jim had opened the door, wearing just his boxers and a grubby, loose sports vest. He wasn't alone either, judging from the fumes spilling out into the night-time air. He actually had the decency to try extinguishing his hand-rolled cigarette that contained his very own self-grown 'herbs' he used to mix with the cheap tobacco, upon seeing a uniformed policeman at his front door, never in his wildest dreams anticipating the reason for the visit.

Mandy had given Doyle permission to telephone him, but he felt that he needed to *see* his reaction, rather than allowing him time to consider the answers to the questions being asked.

The father of Kim and Nathan appeared genuinely

concerned but not frantic. He confirmed he had seen neither of his children for 'about four or five weeks', as, due to his job as a long-distance truck driver, he often had to work long hours, or away, which precluded him maintaining as regular contact as he would wish but he 'had a heartfelt duty to provide in monetary terms rather than physical', besides, he added, 'she' didn't make it easy for him.

Doyle didn't want to listen to his pathetic excuses for his lack of paternal involvement; he merely needed to know his whereabouts at the said time of Nathan's disappearance, and confirmation of thus. And gauging the reception Doyle encountered, and the 'alibis' in his own living room, there didn't seem to be much doubt that the father was not going to be classed as a suspect. Nevertheless, i's must be dotted and t's need to be crossed, so Bond was instructed to appear at the station to make a statement.

It saddened Doyle to witness Bond's false remorse. It was a five-year-old child, his own flesh and blood, and he was missing! He pitied the young mother, Mandy, and her daughter. Their own distraught reactions were enough to make a grown man weep, yet *this* poor excuse for a man seemed somewhat ambivalent, nonchalant. Could it be that he did, indeed, have something to do with it? To get back at the mother for some unthinkable reason? Doyle had been on the job for too long to be blinkered by initial confessions - or lack thereof!

He remembered vividly working on a case about ten years previously, whereby an estranged couple had plotted together an elaborate 'disappearance' of their eleven-year-old daughter who had special needs, to garner the nation's sympathy and funds to help them in their dire time of need.

And the nation did rally round, of course. The sympathy seed had been sown, accruing thousands and thousands of pounds in the kitty to help find young Maggie, the girl with special needs who was tormented because of her label, and the fact that she was neither a slim nor pretty girl.

Maggie's deplorable estranged parents had liaised momentarily to concoct an almost believable story to portray their darling daughter as a victim of some perverse abduction. The two of them appeared on the television with feigned saddened expressions and crocodile tears, begging viewers to come forward with information, imploring their vulnerable daughter be kept safe and unharmed.

You would have to have been extremely intelligent to pull off a masquerade as cunning as this and fortunately Maggie's parents were not: she was found just five days later chained up in the attic of her own father's home! Yes, it happened all too often, Doyle knew; but it didn't feel that way with Mandy. The ex-husband? Well... he couldn't figure him out.

Jim got himself dressed, asked his 'friends' to leave, and went to the station with Doyle to make a statement as to his whereabouts on the evening of Nathan's disappearance. He had been driving back from Scotland and had not returned home until late. His employer could confirm everything.

Bond hadn't endeared himself to Doyle due to his cocksure attitude and bravado. Doyle disliked absent parents at the best of times, especially those who didn't meet their obligations where youngsters were concerned. If it had been up to him, he'd have put the man away simply for his neglect at maintaining regular contact and not being a proper father to his two children. It was all well and good being forced to cough up his pounds, shillings, and pence via a court order; that wasn't something he could control, but it's a different matter altogether when a father acts like one.

A normal, loving dad would be worried out of his mind at the situation Jim's little boy was in, and that's what niggled away at Doyle.

Mandy

Twenty-year-old Mandy had been working at the brickyard for two years as a secretary to the General Manager, when she first set eyes on Jim, who had arrived for an interview for a job she had advertised at the Job Centre.

She greeted him in Reception before escorting him to the boardroom where the interview was going to take place with the Personnel Manager, and she was instantly attracted to him, finding herself unable to stop smiling.

She was always professional and presented herself beautifully for work every day. Manicured nails, make-up, suits, and heels. Her then boss, Ken Nicholls, was proud of his secretary and they had a mutually respectful working relationship. He valued her opinion on every aspect of running the small brickworks and admired her unquestionable secretarial skills. His motto was 'if it's ok with Mandy, it's ok with me'.

Ken was also a JP (Justice of the Peace) and he would occasionally return to the office after a specific court case he'd been adjudicating and tell her little snippets. Not names or things he should never discuss outside the court, that he would never do, but little funny incidents which gave them both a chuckle. One such story she never forgot was that of a teenaged boy who had been caught stealing pens from a stationery shop. His own father stood up in court and said "I can't understand why he did that. He knows I bring all that kind of stuff from work!" The amount of pens that went missing from their very own stationery store was mind-blowing!

Jim was offered the job of lorry driver, as Mandy expected he would, and would be delivering the hundreds and thousands of bricks to construction sites all over the country.

After three years' courting, they married. Mandy felt her life was complete, she'd married the most gorgeous man she'd ever set eyes on. The future was gloriously bright.

Kim was conceived eighteen months later, and Mandy was determined to be a mother; that meant she was going to offer her resignation at the brickworks. She had no intention of taking maternity leave with a fake promise to return six months later, her role as a mother and housewife was of the utmost importance.

Jim wasn't thrilled about her resolute decision, feeling she should have taken the sabbatical leave option; that way they would still be receiving part of her salary. "I have my morals, Jim," she retorted, "Ken knows I'm not going to go back to work. It would feel as though I'm lying to him."

With a hefty mortgage and less income coming in the household, Jim felt the pressure on his shoulders, knowing a new mouth to feed and the necessary baby acquisitions needed, he would be the one having to work extra hours.

As Mandy started to grow with her pregnancy, so did the distance between them. She kept trying to reassure him that everything would be all right, they would make ends meet. They would tighten their belts and maybe she could do something that would enable her to work from home. She wasn't extravagant and she would endeavour to do whatever it took to maintain the standard of living they were used to. She wouldn't buy new clothes because she didn't need to impress work colleagues etc, nor would she purchase brand-new baby items when the charity shops were full of pushchairs and cribs in excellent condition for next-to-nothing.

There was no need to go overdrawn at the bank because their lifestyle would reflect their new situation. Her car wasn't necessary for one thing, so that would eliminate the costs of running two vehicles. She could start to make her own clothes, and the baby's, by buying and restyling items she found in the second-hand shops, or car boot sales.

She reminded Jim of a neighbour who lived just around the corner, a young, single woman with a friendly Rottweiler and a mortgage. She packed in the security of her job to take herself off to college to study agriculture. Mandy had asked her how she managed to support herself and the woman replied, 'I'm having to alter my whole lifestyle, cut my garment according to my cloth, so to speak, but I know I've made the right decision.'

"If Kathy can do what she's done, with no living partner to financially support her, I'm sure we can."

Kim's birth brought love and happiness to Mandy like she could never imagine. She had no idea she could ever feel such an enormous emotion for anything other than Jim - until she held her new-born. Nothing in the world mattered apart from the tiny bundle of perfection she'd produced. *THEY* had produced!

And she stuck to her word about becoming frugal, or perhaps 'careful' would be the better description. She kept the central heating on a minimum setting during the cold spells; she only put the washing machine on once a week and stopped using the tumble dryer, hanging everything outside on the line instead. She showered rather than fill the bathtub. She baked pies and made soups. She bought food from the supermarkets that had been reduced, froze a lot of meats that had reached their 'sell-by' date.

Jumble sales and car boot sales became her source of entertainment and a new kind of social life as she scoured for her bargains, Kim in the pushchair.

She was conscious of not wasting Jim's hard-earned money, not wanting any recriminations from him. She assumed she was being a good wife and mother.

Most men would be proud to have such a conscientious wife and would applaud her efforts to keep within the breadline of their income. Most husbands would love to come home to a delicious meal prepared on a budget, home-made bread, puddings, and vegetables grown from their own garden, toiled by their wives. But Jim wasn't 'most men'; he was embarrassed that his wife had knitted him a jumper for work that she'd given to him on his birthday from a jumper she'd bought from a rummage sale, unpicked it all, wound into balls, and then went to great lengths to re-knit into something warm, cosy, and fashionable on his long journeys in a draughty vehicle.

'Most men' also came home every night to their wives and

families instead of spending the night at some remote truck stop and picking up a 'truck stop dolly' after splashing his cash on a few bevvies beforehand.

Mandy was crestfallen when the penny dropped: she had no idea. She had believed the truck had broken down and had to be towed away to the recovery place, awaiting the broken part's replacement. Why wouldn't she? She also believed it the second time he called to tell her about the puncture on the motorway and was waiting to be rescued.

It wasn't until she decided to pay a visit to her doctor about a very embarrassing and smelly discharge she was having that confirmed her once beloved and faithful husband was no more.

That's when all Hell broke out. How could he have demoralised her so? Her world crashed and burned upon the realisation of her husband's evident infidelity when she could never imagine doing the same to him.

When she made her wedding vows, she meant them from the bottom of her heart. She couldn't bear to think of another man's hands on her body, or vice versa. The man she loved and adored was by her side when she gave birth to their daughter, how could he have forgotten the pain she went through for their family and dismissed it so frivolously?

She despised him for months afterwards. She'd spit in the food she forced herself to cook him and delighted in watching him eat it! She withheld all marital relations until she was 'clean' again and felt duty bound because it was a better alternative than the route of separation and wondering how she was going to manage without his financial support.

The first time she allowed herself to invite him back into their bed was a huge milestone for her, and she had cried afterwards, imagining his face and familiar grunts he would undoubtedly have made with his truck stop floozies who would have been unaware - perhaps - that he was a married man with a beautiful daughter, waiting at home.

These women had no such scruples, she presumed, only too pleased to be able to earn a few pound notes and boy had they managed to score a jackpot with her fella! All six feet and muscle, not to mention his charismatic persona and good looks.

It wasn't fair. It just was NOT fair! She inwardly declared that all married men should be made to have a tattoo on their foreheads depicting their marital status and an extra little ditty scratched on for each child he had. Not that that would make any difference to a turn! Money was money, whatever the deed and disease they passed on.

*　*　*　*　*

Jim

Running was Jim's passion, ever since he learnt how to stand on his own two feet. At first, he crawled as a baby, then he managed to stand with the aid of a supporting piece of furniture. Before his parents knew what hit them, Jim was practically running, his little chubby legs going up and down like a piston to get to where he wanted to be.

At primary school he ran, everywhere. He had certificates and medals from the year dot. He ran in marathons, he ran in the commonwealth games and received a gold medal, he ran at night-time around the parks and empty city streets, enjoying the quiet and absence of traffic. To Jim, there was nothing more exhilarating than the feeling of freedom, running away from the tedium of everyday life. He could escape the trappings of his Dickensian mother and the regime of school.

That's what he loved so much about the career path he'd chosen, the open roads and the ability to distance himself from the constraints and shackles of being in just one place. The world was his oyster and he yearned to see it all.

The job at the brickyard was supposed to be a stopgap

before he embarked on a new life overseas. He knew his good looks and athletic build appealed to the female eye, he just needed a few more readies in his bank account to cover fuel and living expenses before he managed to secure employment in another country.

He hadn't taken into account falling for the beautiful and intelligent caramel skinned Mandy, though. Mandy took his breath away.

He was in awe, not only of her obvious beauty, but her overall presence. She was astute, 'on the ball' and efficient in the way she managed to run the brickworks without taking away the glory from her boss. She managed to convince the whole workforce that every good decision affecting the well-being of their employees, had been Ken's, and he had been sorry to lose her.

Jim stayed on, driving and delivering the bricks after Mandy left, until he asked for a pay rise. He was disappointed when his request had been refused, assuming his wife's former popularity and esteem would be in his favour, but tongues wagged, and Ken did not have the same loyalty and affection for the man his former secretary held. Thus, he sought alternative employment with a company that made and distributed car windscreens.

Once again it worked perfectly in his favour, driving up and down the country all hours and nights. It afforded him the opportunity for stopovers, meeting up with fellow drivers and strutting off into the towns to seek entertainment in whatever form it offered.

Blackpool was a regular trip and he relished it. It gave him the opportunity to frequent bars, hook up with female holiday-makers and take advantage of their bathrooms as well as their bodies, scurrying away around five a.m. to get back to his vehicle and make the long journey back down the motorway to Leicestershire.

He never remembered their names. There were far too many to remember. So how was he supposed to know that he'd contracted something horrible from one of these lovely ladies? And how could he be certain that his own dear wife hadn't been playing away whilst he was working? Nothing wrong with his manhood; how dare she?

And for Jim, that's when the seed of doubt set in. She accused him, and he accused her. Heaven forbid he would admit to straying, she had no concrete evidence to pinpoint him as the guilty party. What was she doing on the nights he was away earning a crust to keep a roof over their heads and food on the table?

She'd never let him anywhere near her until everything had cleared up, but it wasn't the joyous, loving experience he had been anticipating. Anything but: she'd cried for ages afterwards, making him feel he hadn't done a good job, and he wished he could've crawled away into the arms of someone who would be more appreciative.

He wondered if this was what normal family life was like. Intimacy, once the novelty of passion, had waned. Is this the same situation his father felt he was in and left his own mother just months after his birth and he never got to meet again? Had he, too, fallen into the same trap? He began to feel some empathy for the man he only saw in a photograph tucked away in a drawer at the back of his mother's dressing table all those years ago. More than likely the mother he had pitied all these years was just as guilty as his own callous and frigid wife. No wonder his father had sought the comfort of other women.

Anyway, he had a daughter now to consider, on top of everything else. Why she couldn't have given him a son first, baffled him, but at least she had another outlet for her emotions.

Running was the thing Jim was good at. Running away from his responsibilities came as second nature. He made running his thing, running rings around Mandy so that she never knew whether she was coming or going. He didn't care. He had become accustomed to the attention he was receiving from the opposite sex.

He dabbled far too often. He would sometimes experience a momentary feeling of guilt but brushed it off as a mere bodily function. Sex was sex, after all.

He never told his closest friends that Mandy had turfed him out of their home, it was too belittling to admit. He spent the majority of his time working as many overnights as he could, sleeping in the cab of his truck. But then he became ill; very ill and went crawling back to Mandy to ask for her help. Hepatitis B was a huge wake up call for him!

The summer sun continued to shine on the picturesque hamlet of Bugios and surrounding villages, bringing much joy to all, plus it created work opportunities for many. The land-clearers settling for more hands-on work as most mechanical equipment was banned due to the possible chance of causing forest fires. The amount of people who had lost their lives, homes, livelihood in the past years, not forgetting the desperate animals and wildlife, was always in the forethoughts of everyone. Well... mostly everyone. It was beggars' belief to realise that most of the fires are started deliberately, thus allowing the brave volunteer *bombeiros* to actually earn a few euros.

Casinha Oliveiras, the delightful local guest house in Bugios, also began to see a big influx of holiday-making Europeans, some to appreciate the hospitality of the Portuguese and sample the breath-taking scenery, other youngsters backpacking and opting to do a stint or two volunteering their labour on *quintas* in exchange for food and accommodation for a short while. There was almost always something for everybody if they cared to look.

Ethan was thriving. He was beginning to forget that he was once Nathan, as everyone knew him and addressed him as Ethan. And he had Parr. He'd never known the love of his own father. He'd never had the undivided attention of a male parent and he was determined to relish every day. He had Barns, too, who was like his very own shadow.

He was remembering his past life less and less. He loved the fact that it was warm and sunny every day. He could take off wearing just his shorts and tee shirt, with his faithful dog and go on walks in search of something exciting, like snakes, salamanders, scorpions, just like his hero, David Attenborough. One such day he saw a coypu scuttling across his path and Barns ran after it, barking demonically. He couldn't wait to get back to tell his Parr because he'd never seen anything like it in his life before.

Gary had been busy concocting a makeshift study for him in the attic of their home. It was a small attic but it had an outside staircase leading up to it. He'd erected shelving to put boxes and books on, Ethan's collection of fossils, bones, dead beetles, and a desk made from pallets found by the surrounding skips. A chair was constructed from disused car tyres that he'd painted apple green from a half-full tin of paint that had also been left by the wayside skips.

Ethan had been fascinated watching Gary make the chair from the old car tyres, the ones left over had been filled with earth and geraniums planted, to add some colour and a sense of belonging, to the garden.

The nearest school was over 27 kilometres away from Bugios and Ethan was the only child in the whole vicinity, which concerned Gary. He knew the child needed the stimulation and friendship of others his own age, and although he'd been home-schooling him for the last six months, he was nervous about introducing newcomers into their lives.

Every night, Gary would sit with Ethan and tutor him. He would set him tests for writing and mathematics, but the boy sailed through every assignment he was given. Gary concluded that he was teaching Ethan a different syllabus. He was educating him in life. He was learning a new way to live, and he was learning a new language, too. The older generation of inhabitants adored having new young blood walking around with his beloved dog. They'd talk to him and when he didn't understand what they were saying, they patiently gesticulated until he had a smidgeon of a grasp.

The baker came round in the bread van three times a week

and Ethan and Barns ran down the road after him with a euro or loose change in his pocket for half a dozen cobs. His name was Nuno, the baker, but he had told Ethan that he was giving up his bread round because he had found another job, and that saddened Ethan because it was Nuno who taught him the Portuguese words for bread and cake, hot and cold, have a good weekend, and see you soon. And he always gave Barns a bread roll left over from the day before. In fact, it was Nuno who had been his first real friend since he arrived in Portugal.

The temperatures were beginning to climb; already it was in the high twenties. Gary knew only too well, from previous trips with Sarah, that it would get even hotter. A pool was totally out of the equation; even if he had the strength and wherewithal to dig the blessed foundations, there wasn't a cat in Hell's chance of affording everything else for it! The ground, for one thing, was like rock. In fact, it was rock!

An above-ground pool was also an extra expenditure he wouldn't indulge in. He considered an inflatable pool but, again, it tore into his much-needed cash. The only alternative he could consider was finding an old bath at the side of a skip: it happened. And because the local guest house had a pool, sometimes - when Joao had a family with children visiting -

he'd call for Ethan to come and play in his pool. Gary was reticent on such occasions, only allowing Ethan to go when the Dutch or Italian families stayed, never the English.

Bernardino, on the other hand, never harboured the same reticence at allowing the young Ethan to partake in the village activities, whatever the occasion. He was the old school, Bugios born and bred. Saddened that the traditions of his kin and era were fading as quickly as the surrounding villages that he remembered bursting with life in his heyday. He was one of the many that relished bestowing his wealth of knowledge to the boy who listened and watched him make his red wine, his infamous *agua dente*, who helped him hold the bottles whilst he siphoned the glorious red liquid into the recycled plastic bottles.

Even in his eighties, good old Bernardino Simas remembered watching his own father do the same thing, year after year. How whole families would be involved in the olive harvesting, the grape picking: hauling their vats further into the village to the processing mills, chatting in groups eating home-made breads and cheeses, then finally bidding their neighbours '*boa noite*' with their cartloads of processed produce, as the sun began its promised descent.

He was also one of the many other villagers ecstatically happy to have them back home. Them, being family, he considered. After all, his dearly departed brother - Francisco - was Ethan's great-grandfather, Sarah his own great-niece. It was only natural that he bestows his traditional arts to his brother's kin.

He'd been fortunate to have known his brother's granddaughter over the years as she had been a regular visitor whilst growing up, and it was terribly tragic that she'd lost her life at such a young age. She'd inherited that infamous Simas gap between her two front teeth, considered lucky in many parts of the world. The 'Simas gap' it was referred to. Bernardino had it himself, as did his own grandson, and was disappointed to see that young Ethan hadn't got it now, whereas before, he felt sure he had noticed it - when he was just a toddler.

Chapter 15: Coalville

It was July, laughingly called summer, yet the rhythm of the falling rain persisted unashamedly. The sun hadn't shown its face for days and life in the Bond household was as bleak as the weather. Bryn was constantly wet, muddy, and smelly after coming back from their walks or even just running around in the back garden.

He was growing into a beautiful dog and at now eleven months old he could easily be called 'majestic'. He'd been an absolute godsend for both Mandy and Kim, a diversion for their grief and self-absorption. He was needy, dependent, but at the same time loving and attentive. It was as if the dog knew the situation within his family and he would decide to sleep alternate nights in each of his family member's beds. One night he would curl up with Kim, his wet nose dribbling on her shoulder as he breathed like an alcoholic having supped an elephant's belly full. The next, he would condescend to sleep at the foot of Mandy's bed, gentle as a lamb.

Dogs can do that. They are akin to our feelings and moods. They have this superior sense to emotions and can tell a good person from a bad. They can learn from our body language and know how we are feeling. They can smell cancers and find bodies that have been hidden in foliage, rotting for years. They can sniff out drugs, detect bombs, and have an incredible ability to forgive every bad deed ever bestowed upon them.

Man's best friend. What a crying shame that mankind couldn't be more like a dog! They don't cry out and demand material things or give up on their kin. They'll work together, as a pack, the wild ones, like the wolves. They take care of the weak with the stronger ones taking the lead.

Mandy knew that Nathan would know and understand everything there was to know about dog behaviour, he'd watched so many David Attenborough videos. He'd love Bryn! She could picture the two of them running around the playing fields she and Kim went to most nights. She imagined their old trips to Bradgate Park, with Bryn running in the water. The last time they were there was coming up to a year ago. That picture. The last one she'd taken of him, wearing his cap skew whiff. The one that would forever immortalise her Nathan as the boy who went missing, and her - the neglectful mother.

Every day seemed like a milestone without Nathan, wondering what had happened to him. Was he still alive? Was he being abused? That thought tore her apart. Her precious little boy who was so trusting of everyone. She couldn't dwell on those thoughts; it made her physically sick. She had to keep hoping and praying that he was being looked after, cared for, and loved.

It was unthinkable that he would forget her and his sister. She hadn't even taught him how to use a phone and chastised herself often. If only she'd had the foresight to teach him what to do in the case of an emergency! But he had only just turned five, how could she possibly have dreamt that he would need to know what to do?

The police had exhausted all avenues in their investigations and calls and visits from Doyle became fewer and fewer. Peggy Simmons from the TV station had stopped calling as frequently as there was no news to report. It seemed like everyone had forgotten about her son, except for her and Kim. Even good old Mac McNulty had stopped asking if she was coping.

When Mandy returned home from a painful and tense day at work, she sighed with relief at being able to hide behind closed doors and remove her feigned smile, happy to be greeted enthusiastically by an over-excited bundle of joy – Bryn.

If the last few months had brought anything positive to her life, it was the decision to get the dog. She'd thrown caution to the wind and said, 'what the heck', life was too short to wait until it was more convenient, more affordable. A split second was all it took to change a person's life. So many people save and wait for a rainy day, procrastinate embarking on doing something new, until it's too late.

Well, her and Kim's rainy day fell upon them unwillingly, and their 'something new' had been thrust upon them. Now their lives were a world apart from what they once considered normal.

They had grown closer, too. Kim had matured, seemingly overnight, spending more time with her mother and talking long into the nights. She'd stopped spending hour after hour in her room, talking to friends on her phone; instead, she helped her mother with the chores, accompanied her mum walking Bryn, ran every errand possible.

The two of them would relish the weekends together, talking about Nathan, laughing at the photographs whilst huddled together on the sofa, eating pizza, or toasted cheese sandwiches.

Mandy could - hand on heart - never favour either of her children over the other, but Kim had now become her best friend, her confidante, her mentor, and reason for living. They both leaned on each other more than they ever did before, and no topic of conversation was ever taboo.

Kim had asked questions about her father that she would never have dared, before, and Mandy answered her honestly. There was no point in embellishing or hiding anything, the truth was there to be faced and accepted. And Mandy never tried to turn her daughter away from her father; on the contrary, she explained that he will always be her dad, and that he loved his children in his own way, and she could reach out to him when she felt ready. She would never disclose all the unnecessary nitty gritty to her, she didn't need to know all the bad stuff, just enough to know that she and her brother were born out of love - on her part, anyway.

It was two months away from Kim's thirteenth birthday and Mandy wanted to do something special for her. The girl deserved to be spoilt and have something exciting for her birthday, to make her feel that Nathan wasn't the only forethought in her mother's mind, but Mandy was at a loss what to do. She couldn't bear the thought of planning a birthday party, that was just too painful. All those teenage girls, the music, in her house! No. She needed to think of something *really* special.

Mandy talked it over with Mac at work; he had a villa in Spain he told her they could have for a week to celebrate Kim's birthday, but Mandy refused, she couldn't possibly leave Bryn behind.

"Brandy," he said - the term of endearment he often used when he felt brave enough - "you'd be doing *me* a favour. I'm having the garage converted into living accommodation, you could stay in the villa and keep an eye on those workmen for me, make sure they're not skiving and sipping beers all afternoon. You'll have the whole place to yourselves, and the pool. Jean and I can have the hound while you're away."

"Mac, you can't do this for us! I couldn't go away, Mac. What if Nathan came back and we weren't there for him? And... and... and Bryn! He'd be lost without us. He sleeps on Kim's bed one night and mine the next. He'd miss us and I couldn't bear to think that he'd be fretting for us. It's such a kind and generous offer, and I thank you SO much, but we couldn't, Mac... I couldn't."

"Oh, you really are a stubborn Bint, Mandy, no wonder your husb... no wonder your work colleagues admire you so much."

It wasn't lost on Mandy, that hint of 'no wonder your husband'. What? Went astray? Mac had overstepped the mark!

"The villa is yours and Kim's for a whole week, first week in September. Like I said, you'll be doing me a favour just by being there. I'll look for flights this afternoon and if I find some cheapies, I'll book them and deduct the money from your wages at £20 per week. Consider this as an extension to your job description, I think you'll find at the end of every job description in the company staff handbook it states 'this list is not exhaustive' or something like that. Anyway, go and get me a bacon and egg cob from the cob van, my stomach thinks my throat's been cut."

Mandy was miffed! She knew that Mac was just being him; the loveable, accommodating, fabulous human-being he was, but this was all too much! How would her work colleagues view this gesture? She couldn't live on sympathy and people's kindness forever. She couldn't leave Bryn, either! The very thought of leaving behind a beloved family member was just that: unthinkable! No. She could not accept Mac's offer, no matter the well intent. She needed to be more assertive and explain that she wouldn't feel comfortable leaving her home for a whole week, and she began to panic.

But it was too late for any excuses. Mac had found and provisionally booked the flights in the ten minutes it had taken her to walk to the cob van, ordered the food, and walk back to her workplace. Whether she liked it or not, she and Kim were going to be heading off to Spain in September. Now, she needed to ensure their passports were up to date.

Sometimes she adored her lovely boss; others, she could quite cheerfully kill him.

Mum and I stayed up late again tonight, talking and talking as we do most nights, these days. It's nice, you know, spending so much time together. We didn't do that before. Before Nathan went missing.

Mum would never have let me stay up after ten when Nathan was still at home, but now she never tells me it's past my bedtime and I've school in the morning. We love our time reminiscing, and my teacher tells me I should continue to do this with her as it's therapy for both of us.

It's been almost eight months now, I think! eight months, yet it seems like yesterday in a lot of respects. I can still remember every detail about that night, I was talking with my friend, Tamsin, and she'd been telling me all about her new puppy. Well, he's our puppy now!

It makes me wonder why Tamsin's mum didn't want him after such a short time, because he's as good as gold for Mum and me. And I'm so glad Mum got him because he's given us something else to think about, rather than keep dwelling on our own self-pity. It's like having adopted a baby because Bryn is so young and is totally dependent on us for everything. The only good thing that Tamsin's family did, when they had him, was getting all his vaccinations done. That saved my mum having to pay for those. I'd never heard of a Leonberger before, but Mum had, and she told me the history of the breed.

Bryn will grow into a big dog, bigger than he is already and he's a big boy now. Nobody I know has a Leonberger and no one at my school has ever heard of one. Having said that, no one in my school has ever had a brother go missing, or ever heard of someone they know going missing.

Every time the phone rings, Mum and I think it may be news about Nathan, but it never is. That policeman chap, Sean Doyle, was really nice and he spent a lot of time here with Mum and me. He went to see my dad, too, but Dad said he didn't know anything. It's not like Nathan would've known where Dad lived, so it was highly unlikely he would've gone to his house. And Dad wouldn't have taken him either, he was never interested in either of us.

Mum's told me a lot about our dad: things I never knew before. Poor Mum, I feel sorry for her because I really believe she loved him; I wonder if Dad loved Mum in the same way? I don't think I'll ever get married and have children. I want to have a career, possibly a fashion designer, or a make-up artist.

I love both.

Mum's good at making trendy clothes from stuff she's got from rummage sales for just a few pence. She knits and crochets and sews. She's teaching me how to do the same and last Saturday I bought a navy and white polka dot dress from the rummage sale in the Adult School in Bridge Road for twenty pence that was miles too big, but I just loved the material. Sounds vile, doesn't it, but I loved it. Anyway, Mum helped me to restyle it by altering the bodice, cutting the hemline, shortening the sleeves, tapering the waist, and it's fabulous!

It whet my appetite so much that I want to do more and more. I want to create more unique styles and eventually sell them, when I'm good enough of course. I know I'm a long way off my goal, but Mum was very proud of my new dress and now we go to lots of rummage sales to look for things that will be suitable for me to work on. I have to do a lot of the sewing by hand but I'm trying to thread the machine so that I can eventually learn how to use that.

And then there's the make-up route that I think I'd also like to pursue. All the girls in my class like make-up and clothes so perhaps I could do both? I'm not sure yet. Mum says I have plenty of time to make up my mind and go out in the big wide world, because the world is my oyster; but do I? What if the same thing happens to me that happened to Nathan? What if someone took me away from my mum and she lost us both? What if someone took Mum away, what would I do, then?

I did try to discuss my apprehension with her, but she told me that lightning never strikes twice, but she's wrong cos I Googled it and lightning can strike twice and I feel as if I'm almost becoming as crazy as that Mrs. Armstrong who lives around the corner.

Mrs. Armstrong is a complete weirdo. If you don't believe me, you just ask Louise from Newberry's shop! She goes in there all the time and steals stuff, and Louise has to keep an eye on her watching what she puts in her bag without paying for, then she has to tell her son, who ends up paying for it all.

She's so old; probably about a hundred! Mum says she used to be a dancer and appeared on some TV programme back in the 70s called "Pan's People." I've never heard of them! Can't imagine old Mrs. Armstrong strutting about in miniskirts and dancing to pop bands cos she's so straight laced! But Mum says, "you shouldn't judge a book by its cover," and Mrs. Armstrong was once a high-profile person.

She's barkin' I tell you. I was in Newberry's a couple of days ago and she was there too, stuffing a packet of digestive biscuits in her handbag; she said to me "and how's young Norman enjoying his holiday?"

I said, "Norman? Who's Norman?"

She said, "your brother! The one who's gone on holiday in that caravanette!"

So, the insane neighbours in my town think my brother has gone on holiday! I wanted to reply flippantly saying, "yes, he's having a great time, according to the postcards we've received," but I didn't.

Mac had refused point-blank to listen to Mandy's protestations about the offer of his villa in Spain for Kim's birthday treat.

"I'll be just glad of some light relief of not having your miserable face around me for a week. I'm quite capable of making my own tea, you know, and I'm not averse to walking to the cob van in the morning to get my breakfast, either. I'm well house-trained, thanks to my dear old mother, God rest her soul. Having five lads to bring up our 'old man' made sure we all mucked in; no way was he having our mother wait on us lot hand and foot. Besides, I'm not doing it for you, I'm doing it for that poor lass of yours, it can't be easy for her with all the attention she's been subjected to and feeling like she's treading on eggshells around you every day. It's got to be tough on her."

He had a way with words, did Mac; invariably jumping in with his huge size 10s!

Did Kim feel like she was treading on eggshells around her? Did everyone else; her work colleagues, and neighbours? Had everyone suddenly forgotten that her little boy was still missing and that somehow she was supposed to forget about him and act 'normal' again? It was the same as having a bereavement. That feeling of complete and utter loss, the broken heart that felt like the mere act of still beating was wrong.

Mac's words hurt her feelings, and she glared at him. "I hope you never have the same misfortune to know what I'm going through, Mac. I don't think anyone has the slightest idea of what torment I'm going through every single minute of my existence. Every time I hear the telephone ring, hoping beyond hope it's the police with news of Nathan. Every time I lay the table at night and forget it's only the two of us now, not three. Every time I pass his bedroom and see his toys, his books, his collection of dead beetles, his school coat hanging on the peg that he will have outgrown by now. His Christmas presents he never got to open, and his bloody toothbrush in the bathroom."

She started to raise her voice, and her work colleagues turned their heads to sticky beak. They'd never heard Mandy retaliate in this manner before, especially to Mac.

"And forgive me and my miserable face and my unapproachable attitude that makes everyone feel like they're walking on eggshells around me, forgive me for my never-ending grief because someone decided to take my boy away to God-knows-where and is doing God-knows-what to him. I'm sorry that I can't accommodate you with a happy go-lucky smile, Mac, because I'm dying inside… dying! Have you the slightest idea how I feel, knowing that it's all my fault that Nathan isn't here? Have you? It was *ME* who should've been there to protect him. It should've been me, Mac. I should've gone to the damned, bloody shop."

She suddenly stopped shouting, aware that her work colleagues had bowed their heads, as if in shame at hearing her outburst resonate with their own consciences.

"I'm… I'm sorry, Mac. I didn't mean to raise my voice, especially to you."

"Hey, Bint, it's ok. It's ok. My shoulders are broad enough but raise your voice to me like that again and you'll find yourself looking for alternative employment. I don't take it from the missus and I won't take it from you."

Through her snotty nose and tears she had to laugh. Only Mac could get away with calling her Bint or Brandy and she knew that his last words weren't meant seriously.

"And thank you for everything you've done, the villa and offering to have Bryn. It means a lot. Thank you."

Mandy grabbed her handbag and left the office go to the

toilet to fix her mascara. She felt ashamed of herself for her behaviour, shouting so rudely at the one person who knew exactly what it was like to lose a child: his very own first child was stillborn.

*   *   *   *   *

The villa was fabulous. She'd never been to Spain before, and she'd only seen photographs of the villa from Mac's holiday snaps. Everywhere looked pristine, from the front, anyway. The garage was, as expected, a building site. A cement mixer stood idly, bags of sand and cement, breeze blocks and piles and piles of other such building materials.

It was late afternoon when the taxi dropped them off, the workmen nowhere to be seen. Mandy wondered if Mac was right after all and they had gone skiving, or perhaps sitting in a bar somewhere.

She opened the door with the keys she'd been given and walked into the huge open-plan kitchen diner and her jaw dropped. The floor was tiled with white, gleaming tiles. The kitchen was state-of-the-art, and the sun shone through the huge windows, creating an almost ethereal ambience. The ceiling was wood, and the huge beams supported crystal chandeliers which didn't look out of place though Mandy would never have dreamt of installing such regal-like lighting in a kitchen!

Kim was following her, pulling her on-board luggage behind, her eyes taking in the opulence of their new home for the week.

"Oh, Mum! This is fabulous. I feel I should be taking my shoes off!"

"Crikey, Kim, it is, isn't it? Let's make the most of this. We've only got six nights. Come on, let's go and find our bedrooms."

They left their luggage and went hurriedly to seek out the rest of the accommodation. There were four bedrooms, two bathrooms, a laundry room with a washing machine and tumble dryer, a huge walk-in pantry lined with shelves of tinned food and cooking paraphernalia. It also housed an ultra-modern fridge that produced ice cubes, and a freezer.

The bedrooms were enormous! The two girls were spoilt for choice as to which ones they would commandeer. Kim quickly chose the lilac room with the queen-sized bed which had mirrored wardrobes and an *en-suite* bathroom, not giving her mother an opportunity to protest.

Mandy was nonplussed, it was Kim's birthday treat after all, she opted for the white and gold double bedroom with the magnificent view and French doors that opened out to the pool area.

"Mac must be a millionaire to have a holiday home like this, Mum," Kim said.

Mandy considered her comment; Mac was never a braggart, generous to a fault, but never pompous about his wealth or acquisitions. Perhaps he *was* a millionaire? He deserved to be, he'd surely worked hard enough.

"Let's unpack and get dressed up. How about we have a walk around and find somewhere to eat? If those work guys turn up in the morning, we'll ask them to take the pool cover off and we'll spend the whole of tomorrow outside by the pool. Then we need to find some shops to get some food: Mac said there's a barbecue somewhere here… We can get some chicken and salad. Oh, Kim, I think we're going to be sorry to leave this place!"

The early morning sun shone through the bedroom windows of the villa. The whirring sound of the cement mixer also managed to penetrate the walls. It was seven thirty a.m. The workforce had arrived.

Miraculously, Kim was up and dressed in a little floral

jumpsuit she'd made herself (with a little help from her mother). It was a great find at the rummage sale, albeit several sizes too big, but after chopping the legs and sleeves off, a nip here and a tuck there, she felt like the bees' knees, dying to get out into the sunshine.

She went over to introduce herself to the workmen, dismayed to realise they wouldn't understand a word she was saying, apart from one of the guys, who could speak almost fluent English. She asked if they would like a cup of tea or coffee and the guy who spoke good English chuckled at her typical reference to tea. He thanked her but declined. He asked her name and he told her his. He was Christian, his mother was French.

Mandy went out to join them all, taking little bottles of water that she'd found in the pantry and put in the fridge the night before.

As well as Christian, there was Alex, Nuno, and John. John?? Christian assured them it was easier to call him John; the English people find it difficult to pronounce Juan.

Juan - John - was the youngest member of the team, the dogsbody, the labourer; possibly sixteen years old. Jet black hair, long eye lashes, and a dazzling smile when he noticed Kim in her pretty jump suit.

Christian offered them a conducted tour of the work in progress to the garage-cum-apartment. It seemed totally unnecessary for even more living accommodation to the already huge villa, but Christian explained that Mac was anticipating hiring it out to holidaymakers. It already had the structures for two bedrooms, a kitchen/living area and a shower room. The garage doors were going to be ripped out and replaced with glass patio doors; it would let in so much light. It was totally separate from the main villa, and a car port was to the side, easily enough room for two cars.

Mandy was dumbfounded. The newly constructed garage was going to be bigger than her own house back in the UK! How could her boss not want to stay in this wonderful place forever? What made him want to return, time after time, to the humdrum of office life and the cold winters of England when he had paradise at his fingertips?

Alex and Nuno had taken the pool cover off and switched the pump on. The water was remarkably clear as it had only been a couple of weeks since it was last used. John drew the short straw in vacuuming it and clearing away bits of debris. Two hours later, just after Mandy and Kim had eaten breakfast and packed all the crockery away, they were placing the sunbeds at the side of the pool, determined to savour the positive rays of that rarely seen sun!

John was smiling as he watched the now bikini-clad Kim walk tentatively down the pool steps, laughing hysterically at the prospect of throwing herself into the water as her mother lay watching from her sun lounger. He liked these English ladies.

Chapter 18: The Third Morning at Villa McNulty

It was absolutely glorious, this villa, this week away. The sun gives so many reasons to blot away the misery and problems of life. It makes one smile when one is otherwise sad or gloomy. It lifts one's spirits and puts a lot of things into perspective. How can anyone not manage to raise a smile when they see the sunshine over the forests, or create shadows over rippling rivers? It warms the soul as well as the flesh. The weather will always be a mood changer. The cold and damp rain reduces our euphoria making us feel as miserable on the inside as that of the out. That's why we have log burners, fires, or central heating, to warm us. Even on a cold day if the sun is shining, we see it and feel it.

The animals feel it, too. The birds singing in the trees, the domestic pets that lie wherever the sun catches them. It feeds us all, man, animal, and vegetation.

Mandy hadn't realised how sad and depressed she'd been until she came here, to Mac's villa, and experienced this wonderful country. No wonder so many Brits were leaving Blighty in search of their very own Shangri la. How she wished she was in a position to up sticks and find a little doer-upper out in Spain and live this glorious life. But there was not a hope in Hell. She could never ever leave Coalville until she knew what had happened to Nathan.

She tried to picture him in the pool, trying to swim next to Kim. She would insist on him wearing arm bands, of course, but knowing his determination, would abandon them. His shoulders would be covered in sun creams, or he would be off searching for something obscure around the villa, emulating his idol. They would all go to bed, exhausted, though satiated. They *would* do if he was with them.

The familiar sound of car doors slamming and raised voices woke Mandy. She lay in slumber for a few more minutes before looking at her phone, it was eight o'clock. She threw on a long sun dress and went to the kitchen. Kim hadn't yet made an appearance, but she knew it would be only a matter of minutes before she did, having undoubtedly heard the guys arrive.

She filled the kettle in readiness for her usual cup of coffee and opened the front door to appreciate the light and inevitable warmth the sun would bring to the kitchen. She approached the guys to ask if they would like a coffee before starting their work, counting each one. Christian, Alex, Nuno …

John??

"John not with you today?" She asked, nonchalantly.

"He's gone with Miss Kim, to get some bread," said Christian.

Mandy's heart skipped a beat. What did he mean, 'he's gone with Kim to get some bread?' It was only eight in the morning!

Back in the office at Mackle Fabs, the sheet metalworking company Mandy works for, the switchboard was busy. It was Monday morning, after all. Anxious suppliers were calling to say they hadn't received their cheques for the materials supplied. Anne in the accounts department knew only too well this would be the scenario as she had delayed catching the last mail collection on Friday night, thus giving her a little breathing space with the company's bank balance. She took all the aggravated calls with her usual aplomb of diplomacy ensuring them that their 'cheques were in the post'. She was good!

Then the receptionist, Helen, took Mandy's agitated call! She needed to be put through to Mac immediately, never bothering with the formalities of hello, etc.

"Ooh, calm down, Bint, calm down. I can't understand what you're saying. Promise me you'll try and buck up."

Under normal circumstances, Mandy would have laughed

out loud at his statement, but normal circumstances didn't exist under her radar anymore.

"These men you've employed, Mac. Yeah, they're nice chaps, but Kim's gone missing with one of them. There's a young lad here, sixteen or something, John I think they call him, Mac, he's taken Kim! I got up this morning at eight and Kim wasn't here. Christian said they'd gone off to buy some bread, but she didn't tell me, Mac! Kim's thirteen and he's sixteen, what should I do? Do I call the police? These Spaniards don't seem worried, but **I** am! She's thirteen, Mac, she's… only thirteen!" The panic in Mandy's voice was rising.

Mac took a sip of his tea, trying hard not to laugh at Mandy's frantic hysteria. He knew Juan - John, as they called him; he was sixteen going on thirteen himself. He debated telling Mandy the full truth about John or leave it to Christian. No. She should be reassured.

"John has special needs, Mandy, and he's a nice lad. Safe as the Bank of England where Kim is concerned. Go away and stop bothering me and enjoy your time in Spain. Get to know John and the boys and you'll have nothing to worry about. And tell Christian to call me to update me on the renovations. I hope you're not distracting those lads with all your dramas; I'm paying them to work, remember!"

He hung up! He did, he just ended the call. He dismissed Mandy's panic as flippantly as if he'd received an email from some Nigerian Prince telling him he was to inherit a million pounds from some distant relative if he could help him out by supplying his bank details etc.

Mandy was stunned, didn't know what to do next. She trusted Mac, and the lads outside didn't seem the slightest bit concerned, and in fact she needn't have been worried because just then she heard the happy sounds of two young people walking back into the villa, each carrying a loaf of bread and a carton of milk.

Relief flooded her, until she gasped, realising she hadn't even asked Mac about Bryn, but tomorrow was the big day, Kim's birthday. She wouldn't let Kim know that she'd been worried and overreacted. She felt a little embarrassed of her assumption that young John could have done something unthinkable to her daughter. She guessed the lads wouldn't have known why she had been so alarmed, and she must think of a way to apologise.

But the lads did know the reason for her panic as Christian came forward to apologise to her! "I'm very sorry Miss Mandy, we should have asked your permission to allow Miss Kim to go off with John. Please forgive us for our thoughtlessness."

Mandy smiled at him, dismissing his apology. "I apologise to you all, Christian, I hope I haven't overstepped the mark. It's just that I've been somewhat… over-protective of her, I suppose. That's mothers for you," she laughed, trying to diffuse the tension, "I need to learn to relax more or everyone will think I'm crazy."

"Nobody thinks you're crazy; we understand. Look, Nuno has to go to MaxMat to collect the new shower cubicle and toilet later this afternoon, if you would like a short trip out. There is a small shopping centre nearby, you could have a walk round. Nuno's Portuguese and doesn't speak much English but we all speak body language, and he's a good man, I think you might like to see a little of the surroundings."

Christian was right, again, Nuno was a very nice man. Even though they couldn't converse fully, they managed to understand a little. Mandy guessed him to be somewhere around thirty, stocky with a swarthy complexion, and an endearing sweetness about him. He explained, by gesturing the removal of a wedding ring, that he was divorced, no children. Portugal was a beautiful country, he managed to convey. *Muito sol!* He liked driving, but there was a lot less traffic where he came from. He took out his phone and said he had many photographs he would show her. At least that's what she thought he has trying to tell her.

He parked up in MaxMat car park and gestured he'd be about twenty to thirty minutes and pointed across the road to the shopping arcade. Mandy went off, a little giggly at the prospect of walking around a foreign shop, wondering if she would be able to understand what everything was and how much. She'd got plenty of euros and even if she hadn't, she knew she could use her own bank card.

She stood gazing at the cakes on display, they looked tempting and elaborate, which was reflected in the price. How much for a birthday cake!? She did a quick calculation, and it worked out to fourteen English pounds! She debated buying the ingredients to make her own but struggled to understand the difference between plain and self-raising flour, so as a last resort she bit the bullet and bought the strawberry and chocolate one deciding "you only become a teenager once in your life" and it was big enough to share with the working lads.

She wondered whether to invite them to a barbecue as there was no one else she could invite, and she wouldn't tell

Mac that she'd steered them away from their work for an hour or two. It would be her way of offering an olive branch for her accusatory behaviour earlier and a pleasant opportunity to get to know some Spanish people. She put a pack of chicken drumsticks in her shopping cart, a lettuce and tomatoes, a jar of olives, an assortment of cheeses, a couple of bottles of red wine and a pack of beers.

She couldn't believe how cheap the red wine was at just under two euros a bottle, and 13% volume too; the cheapest in her local supermarket was six pounds a bottle!

She waltzed around the shop admiring the different produce on the shelves, noticing a variety of fruits and vegetables she'd never seen before. She thought how lucky the Spanish people must be to have such a vast choice, as well as all the wonderful sunshine.

Now suddenly aware of the time ticking on, she made her way to the checkout and, once outside, she saw Nuno standing by the truck looking at his phone. She apologised for keeping him waiting but he dismissed her saying '*nao faz mal, nao faz mal*, sorry - no problem".

He loaded her groceries into the back of the truck and once they were both seated and buckled up, he began to show her

144

the photographs on his phone.

"Portugal," he said tapping his chest "my country, *muito* beautiful."

Breath-taking views of rivers and mountains, old stone cottages that looked to be hundreds of years old, *"familia"* he said.

"Your family?" Mandy enquired.

"Si, family house."

He was scrolling through while Mandy leaned in admiring the pictures he was showing.

"Oh, go back a little," she suddenly exclaimed, touching the screen herself and scrolling through the last shots until she came to the one with the big white van with the doors open, a petite elderly lady with white hair and wearing a black dress seemingly talking to a little boy who was kneeling, his arms around the neck of a big dog. She studied the photograph. The boy's face was obscured by that of the dog.

Nuno looked too. *"Amigo,"* he offered, smiling. "Ethan, *amigo.*

Mandy nodded whilst continuing to stare at the image on Nuno's phone and felt an eerily sense of calm. "Ethan?" she asked numbly. Nuno nodded, put his phone back in his pocket and turned the key in the ignition chattering away in a language she had no possibility of understanding.

Chapter 19: All Good Things Come to an End

It went without saying that the workforce was happy to down tools for a couple of hours to help Mandy celebrate her daughter's thirteenth birthday. It also went without saying that Mac had given his complete approval and blessing as he'd already telephoned Christian ahead to insist that the four of them do something special for her.

"Don't go overboard or I'll never hear the last of it and under no circumstances is she to know that I've told you. Let the Bint think she's got one over on me and it was all her idea."

Christian liked Mac. He'd worked on the villa lots of times and was always paid promptly, with Mac often sending money in advance to pay for building materials knowing a lot of Spanish tradesmen didn't have the cash flow for expensive purchases.

He'd also forewarned him of Mandy's situation and the traumas she'd undergone. "But don't let on that I've told you or she'll have my guts for garters, I just think it's better to be aware in case someone says something that will have her running for the box of Kleenex and then HE'LL feel guilty. Anyway, she's a good girl is Mandy so what I'm saying is just look after the pair of them, but don't let her boss you about too much otherwise she'll be pestering you all day long. Anyway, how's that new bloke panning out? That friend of a friend of yours from Portugal, is he worth his salt?"

Christian was still laughing at Mac's description of Mandy, his secretary. She was a good-looking woman and had caught the eye of them all. He felt so sorry for her predicament: couldn't comprehend what the pair of them must be going through. He'd seen something about it on the internet, last year, assimilating it to a case of another English family whose daughter had been abducted in Portugal, years ago. The number of children who went missing every day was beyond belief and Christian had often wondered if the parents were somehow to blame in many cases.

He couldn't comprehend Mandy being responsible for her son's disappearance, though. In the short time he'd spent in her company, she seemed too much of a 'mother hen' to have been involved in anything sinister. Take yesterday morning as a fine example when she realised Kim wasn't around! If looks could kill, he would be dead.

Alex had declared how devastated he had been when his sixteen-year-old cat passed away and couldn't imagine how

Mandy must feel at the loss of her little boy. His own wife was five months pregnant with their first child, so he knew better than to dare flirt with their client's secretary, but he also knew that Nuno had a soft spot for her, hence he suggested to Christian to make the trip together.

Nuno didn't need much persuasion, although he was nervous initially. He was well aware that the English ladies were only on a short vacation so there was zero chance of getting to know her better. Besides, he was still licking his wounds from his tumultuous divorce. Rebounds are not advisable.

He liked showing her the photographs of his country which, in his opinion, was much more picturesque than Spain. He would have liked to have been able to offer to take the two of them over the border to see for herself; it was only a stone's throw away after all.

Nuno could have shown her the lovely villages of Taberna Seca, Sarzedas, Bugios, or Castelo Branco, his hometown. He remembered his little English friend, Ethan, and his father who was single, too, like Mandy. But then again, no. That would be insensitive. Anyway, Ethan's dad was better looking than himself, and it would be just his luck for her to fixate on the

English man and he – once again -- would be cast aside for a more handsome face.

John was going off in search of some pinecones and kindling to start the barbecue and Kim had offered to join him. Mandy's gut reaction was to say no, but then she remembered Mac's words, knowing she needed to sever her apron strings and stop assuming the worst of everybody's good deed. She was now thirteen and had her own strong ideas and personality, of which she was inwardly proud. John was always smiling, laughing, and hung on to Kim's every word.

It was actually very sweet, Mandy acceded. Was it her first crush? Was she even aware that John had special needs? They were certainly not evident. Perhaps it was only the language barrier that camouflaged his persona. Whatever, Mandy relaxed knowing that Kim was enjoying herself in the company of an attentive and handsome young man, she'd have a lot to tell her friends back in school next week.

All good things come to an end, as the saying goes, and this trip was no exception. It was Friday night, and they were flying back to Blighty the following evening. Both Mandy and Kim sat around the barbecue they'd lit to burn their rubbish: the toilet paper that they weren't allowed to flush down the toilet due to the villa having a septic tank and not mains sewerage. They'd both been horrified initially when they'd read the instructions Mac had left informing them of such an archaic rule! Into the fire went the paper egg boxes and tomato cartons, till receipts, left over pinecones and twigs and anything else they could find that didn't have to go into the recycling containers.

Mandy was managing to finish off the red wine while Kim was drinking the last of the freshly squeezed fruit juice they'd made from the oranges, tangerines, and satsumas in the villa's grounds. They were subdued, watching the flames flicker, neither wanting to break the silence or relish the thought of returning to their lives back home, yet of course eager to see the dog again.

"Do you think he'll let us come again, Mum?" Kim eventually asked.

Mandy took a sip of wine, nodding, "He has no say in the matter, Kim. We're coming again whether he says so or not. This break has been just what we both needed. It's been very therapeutic for me; I don't know how you feel but I'm really, really sorry to be leaving tomorrow. I honestly don't want to go back. I could live here for ever, providing we have our Bryn of course, we couldn't leave him behind, could we?"

"What if Nathan never comes home, Mum?"

"I don't know, Sweetheart. I swear to God I don't know. I can't contemplate that he'll never come home, I'm always waiting, waiting, thinking that sometime soon we'll get the news that he's been found and he's coming back to us."

She turned to look at her daughter, "I have this feeling in the pit of my stomach that he's alive somewhere, I have to continue to hope for that. I used to harbour that same hope with your dad, that he'd eventually realise his mistakes and change his ways."

She was contemplative before continuing, "Your dad and I loved each other very much Kim. I need you to understand that. And you and Nathan made all my dreams come true. I love you more than anything in the whole world. I don't want to be one of those mothers like my uncle's mother who never celebrated Christmas again after losing a child over the Christmas season, because it isn't fair. It's not fair on you nor me. We will probably, someday, have to concede that Nathan isn't going to come back, but I can't even go there now. I have to keep believing that somebody will come forward with information. Someone must know something."

"That crazy old Mrs. Armstrong thinks he's on holiday," Kim

said, her tone giving away her disbelief.

Mandy looked at her in surprise, "Who? Nathan?"

Kim blushed; she hadn't mentioned the brief conversation in the shop with the crazy old lady. "She asked if 'Norman' was having a nice holiday in the caravanette. I think she meant Nathan. She said 'Norman, your brother!'"

"What made her say that?"

"No idea, Mum. She was stuffing a packet of biscuits in her handbag at the time."

Mandy thought about Kim's words. What had made the old lady come out with that? Could it be that she'd seen so much on the news, or had she actually witnessed something? Had anyone ever asked her?

Mandy's forehead creased in thought as she tried for the millionth time to recount that day. She'd gone to the shop herself to speak to Louise, who emphatically denied that Nathan had been there, and – if she remembered correctly -- was rather brusque. Had she mentioned that Mrs. Armstrong had been the only customer around that time and had been caught out helping herself to a bottle of whiskey? She couldn't be totally sure, perhaps she'd have a word with Doyle when they got back.

"Well, she is a bit scatty indeed. Who the heck is Norman anyway?" She injected laughter into her statement, not wanting to ruin their last night together, "Chuck some more of those sticks on the fire and then we must hit the sack. Have you packed yet?"

"Not likely. I'm gonna wait until the very last moment, and when I get back I'm going to make Mac a 'thank-you' card for everything he's done for us. I've added John as a Facebook friend, too, cos he wants us to keep in touch. He's nice isn't he Mum?"

"They're all nice chaps, Kim. Every one of them. I'd be hard pressed to say which is the best."

"Nuno likes you. John told me."

"And how did he tell you that, hey? In a week you've managed to learn Spanish?"

"Translate, mother. Modern technology."

Of course! All this modern technology. Technology could now ascertain where you originated from with the science of DNA, you can have a baby with the aid of IVF, a fully mobile robotic limb, transplants, rockets into space, the list is endless and yet all this fabulous technology still isn't efficient enough to find a five-year-old boy!

Three o'clock the following afternoon, Mandy and Kim wheeled out their luggage to where Nuno stood waiting by the vehicle he was using to take them to the airport. It was Christian's car. John rushed over to present Kim with a small bunch of flowers he picked for her, and Kim – not having the heart to tell him she couldn't take them on the plane – thanked him profusely with a big hug.

Alex and Christian gave them both a big hug and wished them a safe journey, telling them they must come back again soon.

The journey to the airport seemed far too quick, even though Nuno had taken the longer route, determined to keep their company for as long as possible. The English ladies had been like a breath of fresh air, and he was sorry to be seeing them leave. He unloaded their luggage and set it down while Mandy and Kim got their passports and boarding passes ready.

There was a little uncomfortable pause, no one really knowing the etiquette for saying such farewells.

Nuno took the lead and embraced Kim first, offering the

traditional Portuguese side-to-side cheek kiss before stalling in front of Mandy. She looked at his sad expression, remembering what Kim had blabbed the night before, and took his hands, "You are a lovely man, Nuno, and I wish you every happiness. Thank you for everything you've done for us and making our stay in Spain so enjoyable. I hope we meet again one day."

Nuno hadn't a clue what she said but he grabbed her and attempted to bestow the same cheek-to-cheek kiss as he'd just done to Kim, but Mandy wasn't as quick at turning her head and his lips landed on hers! They both laughed awkwardly, then scuttled away.

"I wish you a safe journey Miss Mandy and Miss Kim. I wish you happiness and peace of mind and when you return again, you will be whole," his alien words evaporating into the ether.

Chapter 20: Time Flies

Three years is an incredibly long time; be it for a child or a mother waiting every single day to hear some positive news. There were so many. Where were these missing children, or in the case of the child, why had no one bothered to look for them? Why had their families abandoned or forsaken them?

Ethan had stopped asking himself these questions, practically forgetting his previous life, his mother and sister and that he had once been called Nathan. His only real recollection was of a woman with dark curly hair, but those memories were vague and he supposed she was dead, as he'd been told on numerous occasions.

He didn't feel sad, though, as Parr was everything to him. He had Barns and he had the love and support of everyone around him. He was living his ideal life and he was healthy, happy, blissfully unaware that he had an entire filing cabinet back in the UK full of folders containing hundreds of papers about him. A 'missing person' cabinet.

And he had the ultimate surprise for his upcoming birthday! David Attenborough was coming to Portugal and staying in the very guest house in Bugios!!! Joao, the owner of Casinha

Oliveiras, had taken the booking and the whole village was beyond excited. Once Ethan got news of it, he could not contain himself, he couldn't eat, sleep, or function properly.

He got writing in his book, listing all sorts of questions he wanted to ask his hero. He wanted to know why there are so many different types of ants, what was their purpose on the planet, how long did they live for? He wanted to know how deep the ocean was and did all the rivers in the world all run into the sea? How could some birds fly high in the sky and yet chickens couldn't?

How could a rat chew off its leg if it was caught in a trap and still survive? He'd seen this happen after finding one of Jose's traps with just a rat's leg there, and then a few weeks later he saw a three-legged rat scuttling away at the side of Bernardino's adega.

He would tell David Attenborough that he wanted to be just like him when he grew up. He would invite him round to view his collection of trophies in the attic, the fossils, the perfectly formed black ballast stone he found at the side of the road, the dinosaur bone that Barns dug up. He felt certain that the man would be impressed with his collection of artefacts and knowledge.

He must also tell him of the time the young Dutchman came here for a fishing expedition and encountered a prehistoric shark in the Ocreza river at Taberna Seca. It had shocked Matthjas to the core when the thing leapt out of the water, creating waves on its approach. Nobody but Ethan believed his story, of course. Everyone was saying it must have been a catfish, even though Matthjas was a professional angler and encountered more catfish than you can shake a stick at! His adrenaline had been racing!

The only resident not to share the enthusiasm for the celebrity's visit to the village was Gary, knowing that a film crew would inevitably be accompanying such a high-profile dignitary, and he was sweating. He considered going away for that period of time but wondered how he was going to achieve this when Ethan was on cloud nine and counting the days.

Whilst everyone was losing sleep, busy making plans for this exciting visitor, Gary was losing sleep for other reasons. There was no way he could possibly stay at home in Bugios under the circumstances. He decided he would have a chat with Joao, find out the details of this fiasco, act enthusiastic and interested like everyone else.

But Gary needn't have been so wracked with fear. The

Attenboroughs, Joao assured him, wanted a little peace and quiet. It was going to be just David and his wife for a weekend where they could unwind before moving on to the Azores. Joao hadn't breathed a word about the booking, it was his grandson who'd let the cat out of the bag and Joao had had the embarrassing task of going to every occupied house in the village begging them not to breathe a word about it as it could ruin his credibility and his future business.

People respected Joao. He'd created a little tourist spot in this remote part of Central Portugal, and everyone had vowed not to let the news travel any further. As a thank you, Joao had promised an afternoon carvery with plenty of good food and drink after his guests had left, and a culinary afternoon of Joao's expertise was never to be compromised.

Ethan would therefore get his once-in-a-lifetime-opportunity to meet the man he revered, and Gary could sigh with relief.

And so it came to pass. The Attenboroughs were arriving two days before Ethan's seventh birthday, but Ethan couldn't have cared a jot about his birthday, the fact that he was eventually going to meet the person he'd structured his whole being on was the only thing he'd been able to concentrate on for days.

He'd pestered his Parr relentlessly to buy him a camera so he could photograph all his fascinating finds. He wanted to look smart in front of Mr Attenborough, too, and already decided on which shorts and tee shirt he was going to wear. He'd spent hours in the attic making sure all his displays were well presented. Queen Elizabeth herself couldn't have been made more welcome.

He knew he wasn't allowed to go the guest house on the Friday night but that didn't stop him from watching every vehicle that travelled up and down the village. If Barns moved or barked, he'd run outside to see if they'd arrived! He was determined to see them drive into the village, he wanted to know what type of car he would be driving, and he wouldn't go to bed until he was sure they were actually in Bugios.

Gary couldn't stop smiling, watching the enthusiasm exude from him. He'd got him the camera he'd been asking for, for his birthday, and had pondered giving it to him before, so that he could take pictures over this prestigious weekend, but then decided against it as he'd have nothing to open for his birthday - *Ethan's* birthday!

And then there was an all-mighty screech of tyres! Gary

leapt up from his chair and ran outside to see what had happened, Ethan following barefoot in his pyjama bottoms. It was ten p.m. and dark, but the lamp light showed a big four-by-four car stationary on the little road, its middle-aged occupants looking a little fraught.

"Parr, it's him!" exclaimed Ethan, breathlessly, "he's here!"

They hurried to see what had caused the noise and just caught a glimpse of Frankie, the neighbour's deaf white cat, scuttling up the embankment, perhaps oblivious to the near heart attack he might have caused the visitors, almost using up one of his nine lives.

Gary asked the gentleman behind the steering wheel if they were both ok, Ethan clamouring to peek inside the window, dismayed beyond belief to not recognise the man at all. In fact, he couldn't have recognised him because it wasn't *THE* David Attenborough after all.

Chapter 21: Disappointment

Gary had rarely seen Ethan shed a tear or get upset about anything. He'd never seen him lose his temper or heard him raise his voice. The boy was a delight and took most things in his stride, unlike his *own* Ethan who would throw a temper tantrum if he couldn't get his own way. Sarah had lost her cool with him on a number of occasions when the little monkey refused to wear certain items of clothing she'd picked out for him. She'd also been called to the nursery to have him removed for spitting on the little girl sitting in front of him during story time and again because he bit a boy on the arm because he was playing with the dinosaur that Ethan wanted to play with!

But both Gary and Sarah had put his bad behavioural episodes down to the fact that he was too used to getting his own way. He was their only child, and it was a certainty that he was going to be the centre of their world and make sure he was happy. Maybe they should have heeded his old grandad's adage, 'spare the rod and spoil the child' - like that would happen! It was purgatory enough to see him upset without any physical chastisement from them.

It mattered not now, he had been well and truly loved and

that was the main thing. His short life ended along with his mother's on that busy dual carriageway on the A50 that was undergoing road repairs. The one Gary had repeatedly asked her to avoid and take the more scenic route as there were constant incidents due to the queues of cars and impatient drivers zooming off before the green light flashed!

It had been a head-on collision. The surviving passenger in the other vehicle had sworn she'd seen Sarah turning her head round as if to speak to someone in the back. It could only have been Ethan, buckled up in the back seat. Could it have been that she was leaning over to tell him to stop kicking her seat, like he invariably did if he was having a temper tantrum? Gary would never know the whole truth, but the entire fault wasn't Sarah's, it was the driver of the red Audi S4, the one who jumped the lights because he was in a hurry, the one with the status-symbol personalised registration plate, the now-dead guy whose widow would never grieve for him after learning he was playing away that afternoon with a former girlfriend he'd reunited with after searching for her on Facebook!

Yes, Gary was angry with her, with Sarah. *"Why didn't she listen to my advice?"* he thought time and time again.

And so he listened to him cry himself to sleep tonight!

Nathan - who was now Ethan. Ethan was so disappointed upon realising that the man in the car wasn't the man the whole village had been expecting and looking forward to. Was it a cruel joke of some sort, or had Joao been misled? Was it another case of 'lost in translation' or had these visitors purposely deceived Joao hoping for preferential treatment?

Gary didn't know what to think, but he did know that he'd have one very solemn boy to comfort over the next few days and also one very miffed Joao who'd promised all the locals a big boozy knees-up for keeping schtum about his guests!

It was quite laughable actually, and although he felt regret for Ethan and his neighbours, he was selfishly relieved! He knew that everyone would have tried their hardest to get a glimpse of the celebrity and post everything on social media, which - heaven forbid - could end up going viral, and there wasn't a cat in Hell's chance that Ethan wouldn't have been in at least one photograph!

The camera Gary had bought him for his birthday was wrapped up in a Lidl brochure that end up by the dozens in their mailbox. They usually ended up in the recycling bins but came in useful for gift wrapping.

He also had another surprise up his sleeve. He'd actually

gone with Ethan on his 'scavenging adventures' and found he was having as much fun as the boy and the dog. There was so much land to explore, so much history that was never taught in schools or found in history books and considered that a metal detector would really whet both their appetites.

He'd asked Domingo, the computer whiz in the village who ordered every single thing off the internet, if he could source a decent one for them, and Domingo asked if he was sure he wanted something so sophisticated for a seven-year-old, but Gary assured him that he was sensible enough to use it properly (after all, he wasn't only seven years old... Nathan was almost eight!)

A dejected Ethan walked outside with Barns at his side and sat on one of the white plastic chairs next to Gary. It was eight in the morning and the sun was obliging them while they drank their homemade orange juice. The baker would make an appearance within the next hour, and they could have their bread and cheese while Barns guarded his day-old cob from the big ginger cat that had been making a daily appearance.

"It's not him, is it? The real one?"

Gary shook his head, "No, it isn't."

"Why did Joao tell everybody it was?"

"It isn't Joao's fault, Ethan. The man who made the booking obviously gave his name as David Attenborough and Joao assumed it was the real one. It's just a man who has the same name. And now poor Joao feels very bad for all the disappointment everyone's feeling, but it wasn't Joao who told anyone. If you remember, it was Daniel, his grandson. So… if you, or me, or anyone else in this village wants someone to blame, blame Daniel cos now Joao has promised a big 'do' at the guest house for everyone to thank them for not telling the whole world that we have a famous icon visit us. He's gone to a lot of expense for the food and drink."

Ethan nodded, half-heartedly, his disappointment was still painful.

"I bet that man does it all the time so he can get upgraded on an aeroplane or train." Ethan said with a tone that would pass for sarcasm.

"I bet he does, too. Well, celebrity or no celebrity, he'll get treated like royalty from all of us, won't he, like we treat all the visitors who come to stay at the guest house but without kissing his feet, so to speak. Let's pretend we've never heard of David Attenborough and he's a nobody because that's exactly what *that* man is! He's a nobody, Ethan, he's just a pompous wannabe, driving his fancy four-by-four, thinking he can fool us. But we know better, don't we? Why don't you take Barns round the village and tell everyone the situation, forewarn them? It wouldn't be fair on poor Isabel to go over taking them some of her home-cured meats for fake people like those scoundrels, would it? And tell Bia and Carlos to leave their dogs out tonight and we'll leave Barns out too so they can be barking all night! Let them savour *real* Portuguese village life."

Ethan was actually laughing. He knew what the night-time would be if Bia and Carlos did leave their dogs outside. And if all the village dogs were left outside at night it would be a chorus of constant barking and howling! It was the prefect revenge.

He couldn't finish his orange juice; he was on a mission. He needed to go round to everyone in the village to explain that they'd all been hoodwinked, and that poor old Joao was going to be the one footing the bill.

He was mentally ticking off everyone he needed to visit and calculated how long he needed to spend explaining everything to them all as quickly as possible.

He'd leave Hannah and Marie till last as they lived at the top end of the road, and he needed to get to those closest to the guest house.

There was Mikolina (the German lady), Hannah, Albertina, Helder, Americo, Isabel, Amelia and Paulo. Bia and Carlos, Domingo, Jose, Daniel and Gloria…

As he and Barns ran round the village neighbours, knocking on doors, breathlessly trying to explain everything, he felt an overwhelming sense of pride and worth, a feeling of importance and need to protect his people.

Eventually he ended up at the guest house with a sickening feeling in his gut. What if he had been wrong and it was the real man after all? What if he and his Parr hadn't been able to see clearly in the dark? Had he just made a compete fool of himself?

Before he managed to knock the door, it opened, revealing a portly, middle-aged scruffy man wearing rather unclean clothes, Ethan noticed. Barns, usually happy to see absolutely everyone, recoiled, growling, his neck fur standing up. Ethan looked at his dog, bewildered to see the strange reaction.

"Get that slobbering hound away from me, boy, or he'll feel the end of my shoe leather," the man growled.

"Please forgive my dog, sir. He only ever reacts this way if he encounters vermin. You know, foxes, coypus, or rats. Is mister Joao here?"

"Oh thank the Lord for someone who speaks English for God's sake! And a damned child no less. Can you please come inside and tell this imbecile of a man that we want tea with our eggs and bacon, not that horrid vile thick coffee! And one could hardly call it bacon, it's despicable stuff, like paper. Doesn't anyone *know* who I am?"

Ethan stood spellbound in front of this rude man for a whole five seconds, relieved it wasn't who it was supposed to be. He ran inside, down the marble steps to the kitchen in search of Joao who he found smiling as usual, making pancakes for his guests.

"Joao," he whispered "it's not the real David Attenborough, that one upstairs doesn't even *know* who he is. He shouldn't be driving either; he nearly ran Frankie over last night."

"*Calma,* Ethan; *calma. Nao faz mal. Claro* he isn't the man we thought he was, but he's still a guest here, so we have to show him our Portuguese hospitality, yes?"

He'd told Ethan to be calm, it was no problem. Clearly, he

wasn't the guest they'd all anticipated; nevertheless, he was a paying guest and deserved the same hospitality as any other guest. Whilst Ethan tried to navigate Joao's logic, he didn't share his understanding. He already despised the man.

Now, karma is another thing altogether. The Portuguese frequently tell everyone to calm down. *'Calma, Calma.'* It used to irritate Gary because he wasn't used to being told to calm down because in his former environment, everything was done post haste. The Portuguese way of life, however, was totally different, they were more horizontal than laid back. Time was not of the essence, and everything would slot into place as and when befitting.

That 'Dave Attenborough' and his hippopotamus of a wife, Sharon, who had yet to show her face due to an indescribable hangover after supping an inexcusable amount of Bernardino's home-made 60 proof *agua dente* and unable to control her bowels and bladder as a result, was packing up ready to depart under a cloud of agonising embarrassment.

The villagers did get their chance to video and photograph the Attenboroughs and would most definitely be posting it on social media. Even the ever-diplomatic Joao posted pics of the soiled bed linen hanging out on his washing line.

The barbecue went ahead as promised, the afternoon before Ethan's birthday, almost a celebration of being rid of such toxic people. Gary was quite saddened to see the ten slaughtered chickens on the barbecue, knowing they would have been running about freely the day before, killed for their enjoyment. There were bowls of salads, rice, plates of chips, crusty breads, cheeses, and jars of olives. There was an overabundance of fruits, wines, beers.

And then out of the blue, Domingo walked towards Ethan holding a large, gift-wrapped item, causing all the partygoers to burst into a Portuguese rendition of 'Happy Birthday to You' which lasted several verses.

Ethan looked over to Parr who shrugged his shoulders. Domingo gestured the gift was from them all, and began to explain that every single inhabitant, every neighbour in fact, had wanted to be included in bestowing this gift to a real Bugios descendant, the great-grandson of Bernardino's late brother. A true Simas.

He carefully peeled back the paper, then tore away at the cardboard to reveal the metal detector Gary has asked him to source! Gary leapt from his seat in as much as eagerness as Ethan when the pair of them realised what it was!

"Please don't spray the flies, Parr, because the bees and wasps will inhale it too, and birds eat flies and then they will get poisoned. The droplets will fall on the ground where the ants live and what if the mice and voles eat them? If all the cats eat the poisoned birds and mice they will die, too."

"Ethan, flies are a damned nuisance, and what about the mosquitoes, hey? They bite and suck your blood and then you're scratching and complaining of the itching! They're only flies!"

Ethan contemplated his 'they're only flies' reply and, yes, they were irritating, especially the mozzies at night-time which he had to admit to searching for the pesky things with the aid of his torch AND swatting them, studying the red blooded smear amongst wings and legs; but who made the decision as to what should be killed as opposed to being saved? He knew it wasn't dependant on size because cows and other large animals were slaughtered for human consumption, but he also knew he would never be expected to eat Barns.

People didn't eat domesticated pets, such as their dogs and cats, and yet it was considered acceptable and normal to kill other animals for food. He was only too aware that lots of local villagers kept livestock for consumption, like goats, sheep, chickens, which saddened him. Was it because the larger the animal or creature made it sadder? Was the death of a fly no less significant to that of his very own dog? He could never imagine, in a million years, eating his own dog so what was the difference? The smaller the being the less it mattered? Didn't every living thing feel pain? Didn't every living thing have a right to be on the earth? Who had the right to take away life?

"I'm not going to eat any more animals, Parr. I'm going to go cannibalism and just eat vegetables because it's not right."

Gary laughed out loud. "Cannibalism? Hahaha, Ethan do you know what cannibalism is? That's eating humans! I think you mean you want to go vegetarian which means not eating meat, only vegetables?"

Disgruntled at having been corrected, Ethan acknowledged that vegetarian was the term he had been aiming for and announced he was going to take Barns for a walk, promptly leaving.

They'd been gone just a few yards, debating on paying a visit to Bernardino in the hope of some of Aunt Maria's homemade cake when Barns ran off to one of the bore holes, barking excitedly, incessantly. Ethan followed, almost hypnotically, noticing a rope attached to the mechanism. Instinctively he began to wind the lever, water dropping as the hessian sacking came to light. The putrid smell of rotting matter made him retch and he recoiled, letting go of the lever and its haul back into the well. He sat on his bottom and cried because he knew what was in that hessian sack and so had Barns!

He pictured those beautiful, fluffy, adorable, unwanted kittens as they were unfeelingly thrown into a sack and lowered into the cold water, no doubt frantically gasping for air until the cold water filled their tiny lungs and their pitiful meows could no longer be heard. It was the cruellest thing he could ever imagine... killing kittens... animals, mice, and flies.

Mandy

If anyone had ever told Mandy, when she was first married, that her husband would have become a philanderer and a child of hers would have been taken, never to be seen again, she would have assumed they were stark raving bonkers, but here she was, a divorcee and the mother of a missing little boy.

It was now approaching the fourth anniversary. Four long long years! There hadn't been a day go by without that sick feeling in her stomach upon waking and her first thoughts were of Nathan, hoping and praying this would be the day when he came home. She longed to feel his soft skin, smell him, and wrap herself around him vowing never to let him out of her sight ever again. But it was hypothetical, she knew - from watching so many missing children videos - that it was excruciatingly rare.

What *did* happen to Nathan?

He would be nearly nine years old now. Had he changed? Did he still love to go off in search of fossils or was he being held prisoner somewhere, tortured, abused, unhappy and lonely? She had debated whether it was better knowing he was dead rather than the not knowing and imagining the unthinkable, but then again, she had to continue to hang on to that shred of hope that whoever had taken him, was loving him and caring for him.

She would convince herself that some woman must have snatched him as he walked to the shop that day. Possibly some woman who had lost her own child and took Nathan to ease her pain, not giving a moment's thought to the heartache she was inflicting on Mandy and her family. If this was the scenario, then she equally convinced herself that he must be being loved by someone and perhaps he wouldn't want to come back home.

Why had no one ever come forward to report seeing something not right? She knew he must be still in the country because the airports, ferries, and even the Eurostar Channel Tunnel trains had all been on alert to look out for him. And yet if he had had the chance to escape his captor, surely, he would have done?

She'd asked the same questions verbatim, and nothing made any sense. Over four years of waiting and not a dickie bird. All those years of unanswered prayers that fell on deaf ears which had left her to doubt her once strong faith.

Kim was now almost seventeen and was the most delightful young woman. If anything good could be said to have arisen out of the tragedy, it was her and her daughter's relationship. Kim never failed to let her mother know where she was when she met up with friends, and what time she would be back; and she was always back home at the time she said she would be.

Her years belied her immaturity, her head was firmly screwed on and she knew exactly what she wanted to do with her life and where she was going. Her wardrobe was the envy of her girlfriends with many asking to buy her creations. The money she'd raised from selling such items paid for an electric sewing machine and now she couldn't stop. She was proud of her individuality, loved finding that special item that she envisaged turning into something totally unique.

She'd made certain pieces for her mother, too, for special occasions such as her birthday or Christmas; and Mandy would take great pleasure in declaring her daughter's talent to those who passed a compliment. There was no doubt she would be going to university to study design, it's what she'd been dreaming of, her very own fashion line.

She was also turning into a beautiful woman, inheriting her father's facial features and hair colouring, and heads would turn as she passed.

She still kept in touch with John as both Mandy and Kim had revisited Spain on many occasions. The garage conversion had been completed shortly after their first trip, but Nuno would always meet them at the airport and return them on their departure.

Alex now had a daughter with whom he was besotted, and Christian was in a long term relationship. All four of the lads continued working together on various projects and they all managed to make time to meet up and go for dinner with the English ladies when they were on vacation.

Nuno had been taking English lessons and was becoming quite proficient. He was initially cautious to reveal this fact to his colleagues for fear of ridicule, but they waved his apprehension away, assuring him it was a wise decision due to the many English now settling in Europe. Spain, France, Italy, and Portugal were seeing a huge influx of Brits, especially the older generation seeking retirement in the sun.

It was hugely beneficial to Christian and his gang as many were snapping up properties that were falling to wrack and ruin, guaranteeing employment for them all whilst they undertook the renovations.

Nuno had pointed out one such renovation they were working on whilst he was driving them from the airport to Villa McNulty. Mandy asked him to stop the car so that she and Kim could take a better look. It was stunning! It was just a very small, bungalow-type building, but the location... Totally isolated and off the beaten track, overlooking a river which had its own river-beach, surrounded by mountains and trees. It fair took her breath away. It was enclosed by natural stone walls and there was wisteria sprawling over an archway, spilling out and intertwining on the rails that hid a secluded and shaded barbecue area. It had a small swimming pool where, to the right, was a constructed shelter where two white plastic sun loungers were housed, a perfect shaded retreat.

"Nuno," Mandy drooled breathlessly, leave us here. I've just died and gone to heaven."

He laughed out loud, "you better speak Christian then, he buy house to sell once we finish modernising it."

"Why on earth would anyone want to sell this place? I would never want to be anywhere else in the world ever again if I owned this," Mandy said with longing in her voice.

He got the keys from the car and invited them to have a peek inside. There were planks of wood in the kitchen where it was obvious they were going to be used for making kitchen cupboards, many already in place. The living room was long with huge wooden beams overhead, two bedrooms and a bathroom.

"What would something like this cost to buy?" she dared ask.

"I don't know English pounds, but euros . . . €75,000 when finished everything."

Mandy's mouth opened wide, "What? Are you kidding?"

"But it will be perfect, and will have new cooker, new bath. Miss Mandy this house be very nice when finish."

"Nuno, I meant that is very good. In England this would be much, much more."

"Then I think you should buy, then you and Miss Kim can live here."

"If only," Mandy thought. *"Oh, if only..."*

Nuno had no idea that he'd just planted a little seed in Mandy's heart. Not her mind, because she'd long stopped trying to think about 'doing the sensible thing', but the little house beside the river had just captured her heart.

The villa's appeal had diminished since she'd set eyes on the little cottage. It was right up her street. Her mind calculating the price she could sell her house in the UK for, they didn't hang around for long in her area. She could buy that place and still have a reasonable amount left over. The cost of living was cheaper, a bottle of gas for the cooker was twenty-five euros and lasted for months. She wouldn't need central heating, the annual house tax was laughable, she had land where she could grow vegetables, there were fruit trees everywhere. Water was cheap, and that little place was only ten minutes away from the shopping centres. So many positives.

But how would she manage to support herself, and Kim? She could start a little on-line business for the two of them, designing, producing, and selling. They could work from home and it would be a joint venture?

Ideas were racing away at the speed of knots; she hadn't even considered that Kim was yearning to go to university and had her own life plans. And then of course there was always the chance of Nathan coming back and what would he think if she'd just upped and left the country, abandoning him?

She sat outside watching the sun set, nursing a glass of her favourite red wine, wishing for the impossible.

"I wish we could buy Christian's cottage that the boys are doing up, Mum. Wouldn't it be amazing to move out here?" Kim remarked as she sat down next to her mother.

Mandy had just taken a mouthful of wine and in her surprise at hearing those words, forcefully spat it out, spraying it over her knees.

"My God, you must've read my mind, Kim! I swear on our Nathan's life I was doing the maths, selling our house and having our own on-line fashion business, you and me, living here in that gorgeous house."

"Lots of other people do it, Mum. Tamsin says her mum and dad are buying something over here cos they love it. And Spain isn't a million miles away from England. We can go back whenever you want. I quite like the idea of you and me doing that on-line fashion thingy, it would be great."

"But you have your hopes set on going to university, getting a degree. I'm not going to stand in your way of achieving your own dreams, Kim. There will be other lovely houses and I'll have managed to pay off some more of the mortgage, and ..."

Kim interrupted, "... and Nathan might come home one day; isn't that what you were just going to say? But what if he never does, Mum? What if we waste a fabulous opportunity like this, hey? Don't we both love coming here? Wasn't it you who said you don't understand why Mac doesn't live here permanently instead of just letting it out to family and friends and he and his family only using it when it's vacant long enough for them to enjoy it? What's the point?"

Mandy hung on to every word that was spilling out of her fabulous daughter's mature mouth, and she wanted to lean over and hug her.

"What if you were, say… retired. I was married with half a dozen kids, and it was just you, on your own? What would you do?"

"Well, if you had half a dozen kids there is no way I would come here, I'd want to see my grandchildren, be involved in their lives."

"Another scenario then. If you hadn't had me and Nathan and you'd had the breakup with Dad, would you – if that little place was within your grasp – go for it, if you could find a way to work, support yourself?"

Mandy took another mouthful of wine, this time holding it in and before swallowing, contemplating her answer.

"Knowing what I know now, I suppose I might, but how could I honestly know? I think it's a case of wishful thinking because obviously I'd need to consider lots of things like pensions, and then there's the language, I'd have to learn the language to cope with all the legalities. I'd probably need health insurance because I don't know how much I'd have to pay for hospital treatment or dentistry if I ever needed it."

"And what would you do if a doctor told you that you had only two years to live? Would you say 'ok, thank you very much' and continue working for Mac at Mackle Fabs, living in dreary Coalville, or would you say, 'stuff it, I'm off to spend the last of my days in the glorious sunshine surrounded by mountains and forests?'"

"Was Kim really only those tender years?" Mandy thought, *"she has the maturity and compassion of a much older, wonderful human being."*

Mandy laughed and laughed. "Whatever did I do to deserve you? Are you serious? Shall I talk to Christian?"

"Mum, after what we've been through, I think we can cope with anything. If we fail, we fail. At least we can say we tried."

And that is how Mandy and Kim came to be the new owners

of River Cottage. The whole week at Villa McNulty had been used as mere lodgings as they travelled backwards and forwards, day after day, hindering the work progress as they asked hundreds of questions about what to do.

Their evenings were spent researching how to create an online fashion business. Mandy had telephoned a local estate agent to book an appointment to have their home valued in readiness to put it up for sale. She would have to seek legal advice from a solicitor regarding taking Kim out of the country when Jim was still paying child maintenance. Would he object? She very much doubted it.

She needed to meet up with Doyle to put him in the picture, ensuring the files would be updated with their new address, should he miraculously need to get in touch with them.

Mandy was buzzing with excitement: it was a wonderful, positive distraction from the last dismal, agonising years. It gave her purpose and reason to look to the future. She felt she'd leaned on Kim for support far too much, but now she was enjoying revelling in believing they had something to work for, to live for – again.

*　*　*　*　*

Kim

I am actually over the moon! My mother has never seemed happier than these last few weeks and it's been fabulous to watch her excitement.

If I'm being one hundred percent honest, I am a tad disappointed that I've given up on my ambition to go to uni to study fashion design, but on the other hand my mum and I are going to build our own business, so it's not that devastating.

And the house! OMG, it's amazing! It's in Spain but near to the Portuguese border. It's also got a little outbuilding that we're gonna ask Christian to convert into a production room where Mum and I can have our sewing machines, tables to cut out patterns. It's already got electricity there, so he just needs to put in some cladding and make it usable for us because we don't want the actual house to be where we work.

"Are we mad or what?" I said to Mum, "Mum, are we crazy?" Because even though I'm mega excited, it is a huge step to take. Mum has to give up the security of her safe job, one that she's had for years, and she loves working with Mac and the rest of Mackle Fabs. Dad's given his permission for me to leave but I didn't doubt that for one minute. It would lessen his guilt for never obligating his paternal visiting rights. I can't even remember the last time I saw him! In fact, the last we did hear about him was that he wasn't well, something to do with his liver not functioning properly. Anyway, I won't shed any tears over him!

Bearing in mind we're packing up and leaving our past lives behind us, I'm surprised Mum considered it so readily, it's an enormous leap because she always swore she would never leave just in case my brother was found.

I think I felt the same, for a while. Well, you would, wouldn't you, if you'd always be expecting to hear something? I used to look at boys in the park or shopping precincts, to see if it was Nathan. I considered the possibility he'd ran away from home because of something I'd said to upset him because I never took much notice of him. I went through a stage of feeling guilty for not being a better sister, and if I could turn the clocks back, I would pay more attention to him, ask about the bizarre things he collected and show that I was interested: but I didn't, and I now know that regret is a bitter pill to swallow. It's taught me a lesson though, and that is to not have any; regrets, I mean. That's why I suggested we buy the cottage, I could see the cogs turning in Mum's mind, the questions she was asking, and how quiet she'd been - deep in thought. We both love Spain, it has so many advantages.

So here we are, ready to embark on a new chapter of our lives. Our house is now for sale with a couple of interested buyers already. We're having to be ruthless with what we're deciding to take and what to let go. Mum has already boxed up everything from Nathan's room, it's all coming with us to Spain.

She's provisionally forewarned Mac that she'll be leaving Mackle Fabs as and when, and I'll be at the end of my school days soon so not even that can stop us. We've already got our website set up and have been busy every night on our sewing machines producing to order. Exciting hey? Tamsin isn't very happy with me because we've been best friends forever, but I reminded her that she holidays in Spain often, so we can meet up then.

Mac, bless his heart, has offered to drive us over when we go and this is brilliant because Bryn can travel in the back of his car; we just have to get his passport details sorted. I can envisage the mad hound now, running in the river, and bounding over the terrain.

And we have our very own pool! How amazing is that? And... a river beach!

The guys have been really supportive and enthusiastic. Christian's chuffed because he hasn't had to pay any estate agents' fees and he knows how much we adore the place. John's really happy because he wants to be the one to show me around and introduce me to his friends. He is so sweet, and I swear to God you'd not guess he has special needs; in fact, I don't even know what his special needs are!

Alex, I suppose, is the one of the four who doesn't favour any personal preference, unlike poor Nuno who thinks that he may stand a chance with Mum but he's in for a huge disappointment if he considers that's a possibility. Mum does enjoy his company, but he doesn't rock her boat, if you know what I mean. She just appreciates him for being him.

Mum has never shown any interest in another man as far as I can ever remember. I think she always held a candle for Dad, but after all the knockbacks she received from him, it damaged her confidence in the romance department which is a shame because she deserves to have someone love her, it isn't fair that she lives the life of a widow, constantly grieving.

I'm sure Nuno would look after her and treat her like a queen, but she said there's no spark there and that when I'm old enough to understand, I would get it. *"I'm practically* seventeen *Mother, I do get it!"*

I have approximately six medium-sized boxes of stuff that I'm taking to Spain. My old dolls, toys and clothes will be dropped off at one of the charity shops in the town centre for someone else to have the pleasure of. All my personal things, like my school exam certificates, photographs, my very first teddy bear and shoes are boxed up to take.

I know it's going to be the most horrendous task for Mum to decide what's going to Spain and what's going to the charity shop, she's a devil of a hoarder. She's got tins of zips that she's removed from clothing well past wearable; a button jar the size of a huge sweet jar. She's got bags of cotton reels, knitting pins, crochet hooks, wool. I kid you not, but my mother even has a box full of Christmas wrapping paper that she's kept from previous Christmases, all ironed to reuse! Sometimes I think she'll need another lifetime to use everything!

She has a box FULL of mine and Nathan's first drawings, every Mother's Day, Christmas, and birthday card we've made her. Cinema tickets from movies she went to see with Dad before they got married, her wedding dress too! There's being sentimental and there's being stupid! I think my mother can be classed as both.

Chapter 24: Spain- This is the Life!

The cottage was almost finished but not fully, which meant that the girls couldn't move in. Besides, it hadn't been paid for yet, which is another reason why Christian hadn't let them move all their belongings in. They would be staying in Mac's villa for the remaining time until all the legalities had been sorted.

This afforded Mandy the opportunity to open a Spanish bank account and obtain the appropriate Spanish residency status documents. Mac drove her into the city centre to assist. She also needed, Mac insisted, a car. She couldn't rely on everyone else to run her here, there, and everywhere.

This fact daunted her! She'd never driven a left-hand car on the right side of the road before, and she was nervous.

"Oh, for goodness' sake woman, will you just stop being a Mandy-pandy, you passed your driving test, didn't you? What is your problem? It's just the same as driving in the UK but everything is opposite! There's no traffic on the roads here to worry you. Just get a grip, will you?"

"Mac, I've never done this before, and I'm scared I'm gonna cause an accident. Let me choose a car and I will ask them to deliver it."

Mac was exasperated, "I thought you were good," he uttered sarcastically, "I'm driving you up and down the city centre like a tap dancer's chuff and you want the poor sods to deliver you a car!"

"I'll pay them for it, I just need to practise on a quiet road before I dare drive it back. I need to feel confident, get the hang of driving on the opposite side of the road and with opposite pedals and steering wheel. Mac, it's ok for you, you're used to it and you're a bloke, driving is easy for men, it's almost second nature, but for me it's bloomin' scary."

After four hours and goodness knows how many car dealerships they'd visited later, Mandy finally decided on a little four-by-four car, much to the relief of Mac. It was a Suzuki Vitara, an old one but with plenty of room in the back for Bryn and groceries. She paid via bank transfer there and then and much to the mortal embarrassment of Mac when the salesman handed over the keys and paperwork, Mandy declared that she would like the vehicle to be delivered, ignoring her boss's despair.

And it was delivered, the next morning. Mac still chomping at the bit reminding Mandy that 'one of the lads' could've driven it back, but she didn't want to put on the good nature of 'one of the lads' who needed to be working and didn't need to be reminded of her insecurities. She would go for a short practise-drive in her own time, get used to the car and its opposite driving functions on a quiet road where she wasn't going to cause havoc.

Mac was leaving. He'd delivered Mandy and Kim and Bryn safely to Spain and was heading back home to the UK. He was dithering with his keys; he hated 'goodbyes'.

"Bint," he finally managed, "I want you to know that I'm really proud of you. Really. I'm sorry to lose you in a working capacity but I admire you for what you're doing. I'm sorry you've had a raw deal and I hope that one day you manage to get some sort of closure. I'm proud of you, you know, and I wish you both all the luck and happiness you truly deserve. I do."

Mandy walked towards him, smiling coyly, and hugged him tightly. She was going to miss their daily banter, their friendship, their love.

"There will never be enough words to express my gratitude and love for you, Mac. There isn't a single word in the English dictionary that conveys how I feel for you. You've been a diamond; you *are* a diamond, and I am going to miss you so much." And then she whispered, "Thank you for absolutely everything."

Kim hung back, watching the two old friends part company before offering her own thanks, hugs and kisses.

He drove away, never turning back to wave, and it was then that Mandy touched her cheek, feeling the wetness of his tears...

It was all done. The house renovations, the payment, the transfer of deeds into Mandy's name, the electricity and water contracts secured, the internet sorted, the delivery of their boxes of personal belongings: they were home!

Mandy had a bottle of champagne she'd bought especially for this day, and a blue and white rabbit soft toy for Bryn. She poured out two glasses and handed one to Kim "well, daughter, here we are, congratulations to us!"

Kim was aghast, she'd never had an alcoholic drink in front of her mother before, "Wow, Mum, champagne?"

"Never let it be said that us Bonds don't celebrate in style, Kim. Here's to us, to our new lives and our future, and whatever comes our way."

Kim took the glass from her mother and hugged her before

chinking glasses for their first sip, "I'm proud of you, Mum, and I'm so happy, but that rabbit you've given to Bryn was our Nathan's, did you realise that?"

"I did, Kim, but he isn't here to play with it and Bryn is; it's a new beginning for all of us. I'm sure our Nathan wouldn't object to Bryn having fun with his rabbit, would you?"

A courting couple sitting in an unlit car down at the river beach looked up to the little cottage illuminated under the street lighting, watching two ladies with the big dog, drinking and having fun. They wound up their windows and turned to each other, smiling whilst removing their clothing, getting down to the business they were there for.

Nuno had been eternally grateful to Christian for the work he'd given him. It had afforded him the opportunity to get away from Portugal, the unpleasant divorce, a chance of earning more money. Delivering bread around the little villages in Castelo Branco wasn't going to amount to much, long term, but it had paid the bills and he'd had no one hovering over him, making demands.

He'd met some nice people and enjoyed the hospitality of the village people who would bestow their home-grown produce in an abundance to him. His van would be full of cabbages, tomatoes, pumpkins, fruits. He'd have so much that he would end up giving most away or, reluctantly, disposing of it in the skips! It was sacrilege he knew, but there was only so much one could consume. He never let on, of course, taking each gift graciously.

But now he'd received a call to return home which had upset him. He didn't want to leave Spain; he was settling down. His dearly beloved grandmother, Rosalina, was nearing her end and Nuno adored her, he felt compelled to go before he didn't have another opportunity to say goodbye.

Christian, however, wasn't as forgiving as his name implied and was miffed at losing a man's labour. They had a lot of people waiting for work to be done on their properties and a man down meant his inability to meet deadlines.

"Well, I understand your family commitment, Nuno, I'm not that callous, but the French couple are pushing us to finish on time and with you being away there's no chance we can achieve it. How long do you envisage being away?"

Nuno couldn't say. One week, perhaps two? He felt uncomfortable with Christian's disappointment, but this was his grandmother after all, and if he didn't leave immediately he may be too late. He was sorry to let everyone down, but unforeseeable things happen.

There was no debate. He was returning to Portugal, promising to keep in touch and would be back as soon as humanly possible.

It was too late, however. By the time he got back, his grandmother had already passed away and he cursed himself for not being able to sit by her side, hold her hand and tell her how much she meant to him. His neighbours visited round the clock to pay their own respects, bringing flowers and food for the family, knowing that feeding themselves when losing a loved one is the last thing anyone thinks about; an old family friend offering to keep an overnight vigil.

Though he hadn't been there to watch her take her last breath, he was at least able to attend the funeral and was proud to see the road to the cemetery lined with the cerise pink flowers of the camellia tree, the rose petals and other flora as he followed the lengthy cortege, joining in the traditional catholic Requiem everyone knew off by heart.

He was slightly relieved that he was going to be able to back in Spain within the week, knowing Christian would be pleased to have a full workforce. He'd finalised his plans and was going to call at one of the supermarkets to buy a couple of tea towels for Mandy and Kim's new house, the hand-embroidered ones with the Portuguese cockerel emblazoned. It wasn't embarrassingly extravagant at only a euro each and he knew they would both appreciate the local craftsmanship.

He was in the store, *Intermarche*, heading for the kitchen utensil aisle when he thought he recognised a familiar little face. It was Ethan with his good-looking father.

"Ethan?" he enquired dubiously. The boy had grown so much since he'd seen him all those years ago. Oddly, he had a flashback of Kim the second he spotted him, then chastised himself for his assumption that 'all English people looked the same'. He was as guilty as the next person for categorising people. He'd do it all the time when he was out in a crowded environment, trying to place their nationalities.

He was quite astute too; the Dutch were usually the easiest to define with them being invariably a lot taller than the Portuguese, especially the backpackers who toured around on bicycles and sported dreadlocks. The French took no owning either, their fashion style and expensive jewellery never went unnoticed. The English were easy to determine, more often the older, traditional Brit wearing socks with sandals, and their casual attire.

Ethan heard his name spoken and looked around, beaming his glorious smile when he spotted his old friend.

"Nuno!" he exclaimed excitedly, "Parr, look! It's Nuno."

The two men shook hands and Nuno turned to Ethan, "you now big boy, Ethan, good-looking too like your Parr."

"And your English has improved old friend," declared Gary, "that was much better than my Portuguese."

"I learning very fast, many English in Spain and now in Portugal also. I need speak much English for work."

Gary was nodding in agreement. "Ethan's Portuguese is coming along very nicely, all thanks to you. It was you who taught him a lot of words. So, what are you doing back here, I thought you were still in Spain?"

"My grandmother she expired so it's necessary for me to come back. In two days I back in Spain."

"Listen, Nuno, Ethan and I were just going to grab a coffee, would you like to join us? Tell us what you've been doing."

"First, I must buy this for my English lady friend, I think she will like very much. Which cafe you go? I meet you in five minutes?"

"The one on the corner opposite Montepio bank, with all the tables outside, and you can tell us all about your new English lady friend, can't he Ethan?"

Gary ordered his large milky coffee, a bottle of juice for Ethan, and an espresso for Nuno, knowing he would be with them as soon as the drinks were brought to the table. He was.

"Good to see you again *amigos, saude,*" he said as he sat down and picked up his espresso to clink coffee cups and bottles. "Tell me, how is your life in Bugios, everything perfect?" He just couldn't shake off the feeling of likening Ethan to his new friend, Kim.

"*Muito bom, amigo, muito bom*. Ethan and I have a new hobby too, don't we, mate?"

Ethan nodded enthusiastically, "we've got a metal detector and Barns is a dad to four of Isabel's puppies. I go to see them every day and Isabel said I can have one, but Parr says I can't, they're all *cadelas* you see."

"What is metal detector?" Nuno asked, his mind couldn't assimilate the English words 'metal' with 'puppies'.

They both went to great lengths to describe what it was and its function, where they went, things they'd unearthed, and Nuno felt a strangeness that he couldn't put his finger on. He wondered if he had missed his country more than he realised. He envied Ethan's father for the very fact that he was a father. It was what he had hoped to be, one day. He had thought it was the normal progression once you'd been married for a few years, a child coming along. But it didn't happen for him, or rather – them!

After several unsuccessful years of trying to get pregnant, Lena, his wife, went to the doctor who confirmed her fertility results were normal. Her husband's, however, were not so, and so she had sought out the offerings of a man who could give her the very thing her own husband was incapable of; a baby.

It had been a bitter body blow for Nuno! He had shed endless tears and felt thoroughly useless as a husband, and of a man. It had emasculated him in a way he never envisioned.

He'd become depressed, angry; he'd been betrayed by the one woman who should have sought comfort from him, not from that of his best friend who was already married with two children of his own.

He considered his alternatives. He could learn to forgive and accept the hand he'd been dealt, forgive the two people he valued most and accept this child as his own, grasp the only chance of fatherhood he would ever have, or throw in the towel. He decided the former, but his wife had other ideas and she left him to move back with her absolutely thrilled parents who had no idea of their daughter's infidelity, believing that their son-in-law was an absolute pig for turning away from his responsibilities.

"So, your English lady friend, Nuno. You haven't spilled the beans yet."

"Spilled the beans? I not understand spilled the beans."

"You haven't told us anything about her. Is she pretty, how long have you been seeing her, is there a future for you?"

"Oh! Oh. Oh no. She just very nice lady. She have nice daughter too. But no, just friend. They make business in Spain, selling clothes. I think she not interested in making relationship with me and that's ok, I enjoy friendship. You should come to Spain, plenty job works in Spain. I see stone walls you make in your house, many people want stone walls in Spain."

Gary laughed at Nuno's attempt to lure him away to work in Spain, even though he was becoming quite the expert at building stone walls. He'd started with a small rockery, and then unearthed lots of huge boulders whilst he was trying to level out the meadow, utilising them all as he went along. What started as one small wall, turned into a very long one. Then another, and another, until it felt like an obsession, this stone walling hobby.

His body had most certainly benefitted from the hard work of hauling the huge rocks out of the ground, transporting them to where he was building, then the placing all around his property. He was tanned and he was muscular. He had a week's stubble that made him look like a model for an aftershave advert in a glossy magazine. He had the charisma that Nuno knew women liked, that very charisma he didn't possess. He could see the same traits in his son, and his envy was pitiful.

"Look, take my number. My boss always looking for man do good work. This my number. When you need some think to do for working, you give me call."

The three eventually parted company, wishing each other *adieu* and promising to keep in touch. Gary felt sorry for Nuno who'd been a victim himself. He was a decent, nice bloke who'd been sh*t on basically, and nice blokes always seemed to get the rough end of the stick through no fault of their own.

Gary himself hadn't deserved to lose his wife and son in that dreadful car accident, and Nuno didn't deserve what had happened to him. How was it that all the bad people in the world seemed to sail through life's dealings, unscathed? Did they cow-tow to an entity more powerful than the biblical all-seeing all-hearing deity he'd been indoctrinated into? What if there was another powerful guiding source, vying for the equilibrium of right and wrong, good and bad? Or did people just make wrong choices, like Adam and Eve in the bible when Eve decided to listen to the snake and take the bite of the forbidden fruit? The forbidden fruit was exciting was it not? Right versus wrong. Choices, choices.

How would Gary justify the choice he made when facing his maker at the pearly gates? It was all very well sitting on his high horse judging the actions of others' wrong doings and being willing to cast the first stone, but he was not squeaky clean himself, he acknowledged begrudgingly.

He looked across at Ethan who was paying the cafe owner for their drinks and thanking him proudly in the Portuguese he'd mustered, deciding he wasn't a bad person, he'd given the boy an incredible life outside the drab existence of his previous domain. What could be so wrong?

He tucked the telephone number Nuno had written on the cafe's serviette into the back pocket of his jeans, doubting he would ever use it, but just in case he needed an injection of funds, he wouldn't lose it.

Chapter 26: Detective Superintendent Doyle

Sean Doyle never got over the fact that he wasn't able to return the young Nathan back home to his mother and sister. In all his years in the police force, it was this case that had haunted him the most. A missing child was every parent's nightmare. In nine cases out of ten the child came home. Nathan Bond was the one that hadn't, and it niggled Sean incessantly.

It was the usual wayward teenager who'd decided to stay over at a friend's house without having the gumption to let the worried parents know, or if they had the gumption, they didn't deem it important. Doyle despaired at the ignorance of the young, their wanton ways and lack of sensibility.

'Bring back National Service' was his long-standing motto. His own father and grandfather were testament to that, and that's why Sean had decided to go into the police force. He'd always been a strong advocate for law and order, he hated wrongdoings and injustice.

His jurisdiction was usually pretty normal, nothing too sinister or out of the norm. The odd arsonist, car theft, petty crimes, that kind of thing. The missing person thing mainly being some old dear suffering from dementia, which invariably resulted in a positive conclusion.

But this young boy, this five-year-old Nathan, had burrowed under his skin, like a cancer eating away at his insides. Not a sighting, not a single clue. None of the dogs had picked up his scent from the end of the jitty in the little road.

How could a boy as popular as the Bond kid simply have disappeared without a trace? Forest Road was a relatively busy road. Cars would stop outside of Newberry's all the time and then, Sod's Law, the very evening a boy goes missing, there's no one around. It was as if the universe shifted on its axis at that precise moment, almost as if a UFO had circled overhead and beamed him up, like something out of Star Trek.

But Doyle didn't believe that bizarre things like that could happen on his patch. He was too old school, dismissing the fact that his own father had declared things were possible, having witnessed such an incident as a young man.

He remembered vividly his father telling him and his younger brother of a time he was working the nightshift at the brickworks in Ibstock with his colleague who was known as Yash. The pair had sneaked off for a crafty cigarette when they found themselves engulfed in the brightest light and heard the faintest whirring sound above their heads. As they looked up, they dropped their cigarettes, throwing themselves flat on their stomachs as a huge saucer-shaped object hovered only inches from them, tilting to the left then the right. Within seconds it had disappeared, whatever it was.

They collected themselves, discussing what on Earth it could have been, but the local fair was in the village that week; it must have been something connected with that, they presumed.

When they walked back to their workbenches, they were met with a very angry Les Bamford, the night foreman, demanding to know where they had been for the last hour! Both Doyle's father and Yash categorically stated that they'd only been gone less than five minutes, not even enough time to have smoked a cigarette.

As a boy, Sean had loved to hear this story from his father. It had fascinated him. There were so many things that couldn't be explained. His father never forgave the company for docking him and Yash an hours' pay as they were adamant they hadn't even been gone for five minutes!

So what *did* happen to Nathan that night? He'd gone to the corner shop a mere stone's throw from the family home, and then completely disappeared. Had he encountered something as unimaginable as his father had, all those years ago, or was it something more sinister, more perverse?

It was literally yards from his house to the shop. The shop that the staff claim he never entered, so how could he have simply vanished in those few seconds? It wasn't logical.

Mandy and Kim had now left Coalville, England, and were living in Spain and Doyle couldn't blame them one iota. He hoped they were happy and wished them all the luck in the world. One thing constantly perplexed him, though. Actually, two things! First, it was the father's lack of concern throughout the whole investigations, but the other was the call he'd received from Mandy relating to something Kim had overheard the old Mrs. Armstrong say during a recent encounter.

Everybody knew old Mrs. Armstrong was a legend unto herself, a bit of an eccentric nutcase, but the locals both patronised and placated her eccentricities. She was, after all, part of the make-up of the neighbourhood.

He'd been to have a chat with her to see what she could reveal, if anything, but found himself going round in circles trying to make sense of her confusion.

"What little boy did you say, Son? James Bond?"

"Nathan Bond, Mrs. Armstrong; you asked his sister, Kim, if he was having a nice holiday in the caravanette."

"Ah, I see. And did he have a nice holiday?"

"We don't know where he is, nobody has seen him. Did you perchance see him in a campervan or caravanette?"

"What? That young boy drives a campervan? Oh, they grow up so quickly, don't they? My Brian used to have one, you know. He and his friend, Nicholas, would drive to Brighton every weekend in it. They had some lovely holidays in that naturist park. He was always a lover of nature, was my Brian. I bet Norman had a lovely holiday, too."

"Mrs. Armstrong," Doyle urged, "did you see him that night? Was he in some kind of large vehicle?"

"Who, Dear?"

*   *   *   *   *

The whole little town of Coalville had been deeply affected by the disappearance of the five-year-old boy who lived in Breach Road. Paranoid parents no longer allowed their children to roam free without being accompanied by an adult. Teenagers were given tighter curfews, much to their chagrin.

Fathers were stricter with their daughters and mothers were apt to wrap each and every one in cotton wool.

People would still congregate in clusters in supermarkets dissecting the ins and outs, finger pointing and blaming; some declaring adamantly that they would never let their youngsters out of sight for a second, whilst others stated that children shouldn't have to feel as if they're living in fear every day, they should be able to do a simple errand like going to the local shops.

The school gates were now crowded every morning and afternoon with self-righteous parents clambering to be seen ensuring the safe delivery and collection of their precious offspring. It was almost like 'after the horse has bolted' but if it saved another child from being taken away and another family enduring the nightmare, then so be it.

The lampposts no longer were festooned with colourful 'Missing' posters showing Nathan Bond's smiling, innocent face, immortalised thereinafter as 'that boy who went missing', now just scraps of paper remaining, held on by white plastic tags. Most had forgotten anyway; someone else's problem not theirs. 'I'm all right, Jack'.

"Mum, do you remember me telling you about that new dress shop that opened in Leicester. The one who ordered six pairs of our psychedelic dungarees?"

Mandy's mouth was full of pins as she was concentrating on pinning a skirt onto a bodice, "Mmm, I do, why?"

"They've placed another order for six more *AND* they've sent me a sketch of a summer dress they want us to produce. I like it, it's definitely something we'd wear. Here, look."

She showed her mother the sketch the shop had emailed over, and Mandy agreed it was definitely something they would both wear. The perfect, cool, floaty summer dress, ideal for most shapes and sizes, and ages!

"We could obviously put our own stamp on this, lower the neckline slightly, and possibly add cropped sleeves for those who don't wanna show their batwings, like you."

"You cheeky mare, I don't have batwings!"

"'Oh to see ourselves as others see us' springs to mind, isn't that one your usual anecdotes? Only kidding, mother dearest, only kidding, but this style is timeless, and we've got some great patchwork-look fabric that I think would suit this style. What do you think?"

Mandy removed the pins from her mouth. "Let me see again."

"Erm… also they want to know if they can either come over and see our production facilities to discuss bulk ordering or could we go over there to chat about how we can best accommodate them. They're opening another franchise somewhere else imminently and they want to have a stock of our stuff. They want me to take some samples. What do you think?"

"They want you to take some samples. Have you already agreed to go?"

"No, of course I haven't. I wouldn't agree to anything before running it by you. I don't really like the idea of them coming here though, they might think we couldn't cope, and perhaps we can't, I haven't any idea of numbers they're thinking about."

"I don't like the sound of giving them samples, Kim. That implies they want them for nothing and we're not a charity; and if you go back to the UK that will be… what? A week? I won't be able to get everything we've got on order sewn up,

216

packed up, sent off, on my own. We're already committed for the next few weeks. Oh, I don't know! We'll need to think about it."

Kim was sitting next to Nuno who was driving her to the coach station where she would embark on the coach taking her to the airport. He was insistent on taking her to the airport, but Kim was just as insistent on making her own way. Bryn sat in the back seat of the car, oblivious to the fact that one of his family members would be going away for a week, his head hanging out of the window.

Even though it was just a ten-minute drive to the coach station, Nuno didn't feel comfortable dropping her off there. He sat in the car, waiting until he could clearly see her boarding, and then the coach drive away. He knew Mandy would be alone in the cottage and contemplated asking her out for dinner; perhaps she would welcome his company. They'd always had a mutual enjoyable friendship. Or was that all it was, an enjoyable and comfortable friendship?

He was boring, wasn't he? He hadn't the charisma or sex appeal that women wanted. He was just your average 'boy next door', the type to be relied upon to deliver their daughters safely to bus stations, someone to have a pleasant evening meal with at no cost to themselves. The dependable bit of muscle who would come running at your beck and call when the gas wasn't working properly for the shower. The one who mended the plugs because the wiring was different to that of the English. The soft lad that came over to saw the overhanging branches of the enormous fir trees that were touching the electric cables. The boring Nunos of the world.

He watched Bryn out of his mirror, his ears blowing with the force of the speed he was travelling, his mouth wide open and his huge tongue lolling out. If only people were as loving and loyal as dogs, he thought inwardly. Why do humans put so much emphasis on sex and chemistry? Swans will choose a mate and they will remain together forever, like lobsters and so many others, otters, beavers, wolves!

What was the fundamental difference between man and animal that created so many problems? Of course, he knew the rules didn't apply to primates or dolphins, but surely mankind had big enough brains and consciences to realise the pain of betrayal?

He approached the slipway to Mandy's cottage, noticing the lights in the kitchen. He considered just opening the back door of his vehicle and letting Bryn run home and driving off, not bothering to let her know her daughter was safely on board the coach, but he was feeling sorry for himself. He was feeling very neglected and frustrated, a voice that was going unheard because nobody cared enough to listen. One of those silent voices of the suicides left hanging from some motorway bridge, or the voice of the broken victim who had reached the point of no return. His silenced voice! Had he now stooped that low that he thought about hurting his friend, the woman he liked but knew he was going to get nowhere nearer than the obligatory hug and kiss on the cheek that she bestowed upon any kindly friend or neighbour? Was he about to forsake his morals, his upbringing, and shame his family? Did those things actually matter, anyway?

Bryn ran to the front door then turned to look back at Nuno, cocking his head to one side. He began to growl, lowering his body closer to the ground, staring at him, guarding the door and his mistress inside.

And then Nuno understood exactly why people choose dogs over people for the reasons he'd only minutes earlier told himself; because they were loving and more loyal than the disgusting piece of trash he had very nearly become! Indeed, why was putting so much emphasis on sex and chemistry so important? Mandy and Kim were his friends, and he knew he was a valued friend and that's all he ever would be, so he had to take a step back and accept that. Bryn was a big dog now and Nuno knew there wasn't a chance he was going to get by him. The dog must've picked up his evil thoughts and wasn't going to let anything bad happen to his family.

Nuno nodded, knowing he'd now lost the dog's trust, so he called Mandy on the phone to say he'd dropped Kim off at the coach station and Bryn at her house then drove away, licking his wounds.

Meanwhile, Kim sat in her seat on the plane sharing a row with two young guys heading for London, it was the Fashion Week: one a hairdresser/groomer, the other a make-up artist. She was in her element, feeling liberated travelling on her own for the first time.

Ben, it transpired, was the hairdresser/groomer; Po - his colleague, the make-up artist. The three never drew breath the whole length of the flight. They talked incessantly about their own passions of creativity and their aspirations. Ben also originated from Leicestershire, he told her, but moved to London to further his career. Po was from Taiwan and had travelled the world before he too settled in London. The pair of them had been fortuitous to work in the beauty industry and glorify the mega rich and famous along the way, earning an enviable living.

Kim was agog. These two guys, not so many years older than herself, had reached the dizzy heights she had once aspired to, but felt as though she'd forsaken that opportunity when she opted out of going to university.

Ben laughed at her. "I got chucked out of school when I was a kid and Po, here, well, he didn't have the schooling you and I had, and he's had to learn a totally different way of life and language to get to where he is today. We have both said that success isn't about schooling or certificates, it's all about personality, it's how you sell yourself and how you interact with those you're working with. It all boils down to the luck of the draw. Give us a gleg of some of your designs."

Kim was apprehensive to show her creations to the two who were going to be at the London Fashion Week where superstars were going to be bejewelled in magnificent gowns that would cost more than her mother had sold their house for; photographed and displayed on TV, social media, high profile magazines. Her humble designs were laughable in comparison to what they were used to! But, to Kim's surprise, Ben didn't laugh or scoff at her portfolio. On the contrary, he studied them all, turning each A4 sheet, studiously.

"How old did you say you are?"

"I'm sixteen but I'll be seventeen soon."

"And you're going to take this to a woman who has a franchise in Leicester?"

"Yes."

"Hmm. I'd like to say don't and let me take them with me to Artur, a friend of ours who's always on the lookout for the kind of thing you're doing. He loves the flamboyant colours you use in your designs, the *avant garde* look; and this one here, the Greek-goddess style with the gold appliqué on the shoulder, it reminds me of a photo shoot I did years ago with that actress who married that actor from that film... Come on, Po, help me out here..."

Kim was breathless listening to her fellow passengers praise her work, her head spinning; she couldn't wait to land and phone her mum.

When the plane began its descent, phone numbers and email addresses had been exchanged and they had all promised to keep in touch. She envied their lifestyle and the opportunities of both meeting and working with top celebrities, the functions they were commissioned to attend, the money they were earning!

The coach from Luton to Leicester had been delayed an hour which afforded Kim the opportunity to make a quick phone call to her mother, hardly managing to draw breath.

"Let's not get above our station, Sweetheart. We're only just touching the surface. I doubt we'll ever reach the dizzy heights of creating anything that's going to end up on the red carpet at Fashion Week but it's lovely to know you had such nice, encouraging people sitting next to you, and one of them was from Leicestershire, too, you say?"

"Yeah, the hairdresser groomer one. He used to live in Stoneygate, but he now lives in London. They were both so easy to talk to, they made me feel as though everything was possible. Anyway, everyone's boarding the bus now, Mum, so I'll call you again when I'm at Tamsin's."

Manikin was the online business name they'd come up with, assimilated to mannequin. It was the best they had been able to come up with and one that they both agreed on. It also resembled both their names - a mixture of Mandy and Kim. They'd both chuckled when they had finally decided on

Manikin, after ensuring no one else had bagged it first.

Tamsin and her mum had agreed to collect Kim from Leicester bus station once they'd received confirmation of her arrival time, ten p.m., but Kim's phone battery had died and she hadn't been able to make the call whilst on route and so when she arrived in Leicester and her suitcase had been unloaded, she tried to find an electric outlet to charge her phone up just enough to enable her to make a call.

She was instantly reminded of the doom, gloom, wet and cold weather that she and her mother had been lucky to escape from. The down-and-outs, druggies and drunkards pestered her for 'any spare change', with one tugging at her trouser leg and practically pulling her to the ground. She swiped his grubby hand away and then noticed the eyes, the nose, the crooked grin of her father! Had he fallen so far that his life was reduced to this? It was beyond her comprehension.

Her first reaction was to run, to disown the hand that had once caressed her and wiped away her baby tears, the hand that spoon fed her pretending the spoon was an aeroplane, circling it in front of her open mouth, teasing her.

"Dad!" she whispered; she didn't want anyone within earshot to hear her admission. "Dad, is that you?"

Kim was mortified. It had been years since she last laid eyes on her dad, but she knew it was him all right! His skin was yellow, and he had missing teeth. His eyes were sunken and black, he had a beard, and he smelt like he'd slept in the same clothes for years. Oh, how she wished she'd never seen him and could dismiss that slight pull on her heartstrings. He was family, her father, she couldn't just turn her back on the pathetic creature he'd become, could she?

She bent down to look at him. "Dad, it's me… It's Kim."

"Got any snout, Love? A couple a quid to spare?" He clearly didn't know who she was.

"Watch my suitcase for a minute, Dad, I'm going to get you some cigarettes from that machine over by the foyer. Don't move, I'll be back in sec. I promise."

Chapter 28: Dilemma

"I can't believe the scum bag did that to you, Kim. I'm so sorry you had to experience that, but don't beat yourself up over it, Sweetheart. I'm sure I might have done exactly the same if I'd been in your shoes; hey, at least you had your phone and passport and handbag still with you! Don't worry about the merchandise, I've already spoken to the clients, and they seem pretty understanding, I guess. What did the police have to say about it? I'm assuming you did notify the police, Kim?"

"Mum, how could I have called the police on Dad? You should've seen him; he was almost unrecognisable! He looked like a tramp; in fact he *is* a tramp! I haven't told Tamsin or her mother, how could I? I just told them someone robbed me of my luggage. Tamsin's mum's sorted out some clothes for me to wear but I feel awful cos I don't wear leggings anymore, and I'm gonna have to go to Marks and Spencer's to get some decent underwear cos there is no way I'm wearing anyone else's knickers!"

"Ok I get that, Kim, but just remember how many people sleep in hotels or hospital beds and the sheets are washed hundreds of times, just like Tamsin's underwear, you see. But don't get going overboard buying more than you can wash out every day, ok? You've still got your iPad with your designs so not all has been lost and I've been busy making up some more orders so they're still getting everything, it just means it will arrive by courier, instead. Erm… did he look really bad, Kim, you know… your dad?"

"He didn't know me, Mum. He didn't recognise me even though I told him who I was. Sorry, Mum."

"Bryn met a new friend today; I saw him over the wall dancing around and running after a fox cub. You should've seen the pair of them playing together. It was wonderful. A bit odd though, a fox cub all on its own. I wonder where its mother is and what it was doing by the river all alone," Mandy replied, putting an end to the previous subject.

"Kim, it's Ben. Shown some of your stuff to Artur. He wants to see more. When are you back in London? Can we meet up?"

Kim was happy to receive some good news, the episode with her father had deflated her. She was saddened to see him in such dire circumstances and at the same time livid that he'd ran off with her suitcase, the samples they'd worked so hard to get ready, and a weeks' worth of clothing she needed to replace.

The franchise people were none-too-happy despite Mandy phoning ahead and putting them in the picture; they'd been relying on her and failed to understand their reasons for not involving the police. Theft was theft, no matter what promises Mandy made to have some more produced and sent over, the momentum was lost. Ms. Devaney had been let down and she wasn't one for giving in lightly to second chances.

Kim did meet up with Ben upon her return to Luton to catch the flight back to Spain, she had hours to kill so took a detour. They sat drinking coffee in a cafe close to St. Pancras train station where Kim relayed the details of her luggage snatch.

"Well, I totally understand your client wondering why you didn't call the police, the police station isn't too far from St. Margaret's; I'm sure they'd have been over within minutes. Why did you let the creep get away, especially considering you'd gone to get him a packet of fags?"

She liked Ben and his easy, laid-back demeanour. She felt comfortable in his knowing presence, feeling she was able to tell him everything and he'd judge most definitely but in a constructive way, not belittling: so she did exactly that and practically told him her life history.

Ben laughed, "I'm telling you now, Kimmy, if that was my

dad, I'd *definitely* have called the police! Serve the bar-steward right for how he's treated you and your poor mum. You missed your perfect opportunity for revenge."

They ordered another coffee. "And sh*t happens when you're travelling. I was doing the Fashion Week in Milan one year and stupidly left all my hairdressing equipment bag on the pissin' train! Of course, it was never handed in and I had to beg, steal and borrow equipment any which way I could cos I'd got a whole load of celebs to beautify. No one wants to hear excuses or apologies in the world of fashion! Oh, and by the way, I'm sorry about that horrible business with your little brother. I do remember seeing something about it on the tele years ago. So they never found anything at all?"

Kim shook her head, remembering all the times she'd been asked the same question, recalling the nights she and her mother scoured the streets, the parks, the local beauty spots hoping yet not hoping to find him.

"I have a younger sister with special needs, and I suppose – being being classed as vulnerable – we all used to be overprotective of her. Oh, we're not now. She's grown up and very independent, *AND* very astute! She catches planes, trains, and buses all by herself and she's fearless, I tell you."

Kim could feel Ben's pride as he talked about his sister. "We don't even worry about her getting in a car with someone she doesn't know, either, cos I remember one time she had come to London from Leicester, and we had arranged to meet in a bar. I would normally meet her off the train, but I'd been working and couldn't get there in time, so I gave her directions, the number of the bus to catch and told her to meet us at the bar. Well, apparently, as she was walking to the bus stop, some young chap in a fancy sports car pulled up at the side of her, gave her a load of compliments and offered her lift. I was impressed, it's usually the sports car that lures them, but my 'skin and blister' informed him that she didn't know him and she was quite capable of making her own way, thank you very much."

"Wow, that was mature of your sister. See, that's what Mum and I don't get, because Nathan wouldn't have gone off with anybody he didn't know, and surely if he was grabbed, he would've screamed, and someone would've heard him?"

"Perhaps it *was* someone he knew then?"

Kim shook her head again. "The police would have established that, they have been amazing, they interviewed absolutely everybody we know. They searched houses, they checked phone records, they even searched our garden for freshly dug soil; Mum was horrified – as if we had anything to do with his disappearance! The only thing I can think of is that he's dead and we'll never know what happened to him, but Mum doesn't share my thoughts. She's convinced he's still alive and that one day he'll be found."

"You never know, Kimmy. Look, your train will be leaving in fifteen minutes, best get a move on. Like I said, Artur was impressed with your designs, and he'd like you to send some more. You can email them to me, date them and put your name on so you can be assured he won't steal them, not that he's inclined to do that but Artur likes a little drink... No, I'll rephrase that, Artur likes a *lot* to drink, and sometimes he'll print something off and assume it's something he's created. He usually produces his best work after a bottle of *vinho*."

She only just managed to leap on the train seconds before the door closed! She found her allocated seat and flopped into it, her face flushed, a broad smile on her face. Ben was gorgeous. Ben was 'totes fanciable'. Ben was already in a relationship with Po!

Manikin had received their very first commission from Artur. He wasn't going to reveal details other than it was for a very high-profile Hollywood actress and he'd send Kim the measurements, fabric specifications, and a timeframe. He'd always lusted after the Greek-goddess style gown with the gold appliqué on the shoulder, but his client wanted a more contemporary look.

Mandy and Kim were beyond excited, this was their first big deal after losing out on the Leicester franchise and were constantly backwards and forwards corresponding with Artur. His client wanted the style of the Greek look but not the colour, she wanted to stand out from the crowd in a rainbow of brilliance.

The two women sketched, stitched, dyed fabrics, played with trimmings, edgings, fastenings, etc. Mandy made a full prototype of the most divine duck-egg blue, apple-green, pink, yellow and orange hues all seeping into each other in a long flowing gown that did indeed look like a rainbow swaying in a breeze, reflected by the sun.

"Try it on, Kim, let's see what you look like in it."

Kim had braided her long blonde hair at the nape of her neck to finish off the look, and she looked stunning. Mandy took a sharp intake of breath as she knelt on the floor adding pins to hem, realising how beautiful her daughter had become. She couldn't have looked more beautiful if it was her wedding gown she was trying on and she was surprised that she'd never noticed just how perfect her daughter was with her flawless complexion, her almost golden eyes and long lashes. She had blinked and her daughter had become a woman.

Mandy suddenly acknowledged that her daughter hadn't even got a boyfriend and living as remotely as they did, the chances of her meeting a nice young man were slim, unless she ventured into the city centre and frequented the nightlife scene. It wasn't natural that she stayed at home day in, day out, stooped over a sewing machine, surrounded by patterns, fabrics, pins, cottons, and dog hair. If she was still living in the UK she would have a gang of girlfriends to pal around with. Ought Mandy to suggest they both go out for something to eat one night then move on to the bars later?

"Mum, I'm fine, honestly. To be honest I don't much care for going into the city centre at the moment. There are too many loud-mouthed drunken tourists about. John and I are meeting up with a crowd of people next Saturday afternoon anyway. We're going to the swimming pool first and then to the old pizza place, so my social life isn't quite as dormant as you think it is. John's good company, he looks after me and he's got a nice variety of friends. I'm happy. Stop possessing."

Kim was right, she had a maturity that always belied her years. And John couldn't be faulted in the slightest. He'd even passed his driving test and had bought himself a little car. He was every mother's dream boyfriend for their daughter in almost every respect but one: the fact that he did have special needs and had been known to have meltdowns. He'd latched on to Kim when he first set on eyes on her all those years ago and it was so sweet; but John felt possessive over her and could get jealous if anyone else paid her too much attention, especially if he was being neglected as a result. Mandy hoped that things would never turn unsavoury between them because John was now a man. He was muscular through lifting heaving building materials, and to anyone observing, John was besotted!

He'd been like a bear with a sore head whilst Kim had gone to England that time, constantly texting to ask what date she was returning; but no matter what mood he was ever in, Kim always managed to pacify him with a quick hug reminding him he was her bestie forever. It always worked, too, for now.

Nuno had been keeping a relatively low profile from River Cottage as much as not to draw attention to that fact. He knew the dog mistrusted him now and Mandy had asked him if he knew anyone who was available to build some stone walls and steps to the rear of their swimming pool, giving access to the upper terrain where she could sit on an evening to admire the view across the river. She'd unearthed a ton of boulders that she considered ideal for the project. Her first feeble attempt at digging out the base and placing a few choice rocks was pitiful, deciding her dainty hands were born to sew – not build – and now the weeds had grown over everything she'd started.

The job was well within Nuno's capabilities, but he cowardly declined, telling her he had a good friend just across the border who was expert at such a skill; he'd get in touch with him to see if he was available and willing to do it. Mandy agreed to leave it with him, there was no hurry.

*　*　*　*　*

"Ethan, we might have to go away for a few days to do some wall building for a friend of Nuno's," Gary informed him one evening as they sat eating dinner. "It's just in Spain, not far away, but I'll have to spend a few days over there. Fancy a little trip, or would you prefer to stay with Bernardino or Joao at the guest house?"

"Spain. Have I been there?" he asked, the word playing in his memory box as if he'd heard of it before.

"We've driven through it a few times when we came over on the ferry, but you were too young to remember and most of the time you were always fast asleep on your mum's lap," he lied.

"We'll drive over in the campervan, that way we'll have our own accommodation. You should bring the metal detector too. Nuno says we should set out on Sunday afternoon so that we can be there by late evening. He's going to meet us as soon as we arrive at the Spanish border. Oh blimey! We won't be able to take Barns though, he's not got a passport. I'll have to ask someone in the village if they'll come over and feed him."

Ethan tried to recall being on this mother's lap, many of the village people talked about her and of the family. He knew that Bernardino was some kind of great-uncle but didn't understand the whole lineage thing. Try as he might, he could not picture *this* woman as his mother. He'd gone through a stage of asking questions about her, wanting to see photographs, and Gary had shown him. He'd studied the photographs, recognising himself then touching his front teeth to feel for the gap – like in the pictures – that was no longer there. He saw his younger self enveloped by a pretty, laughing, young woman who had that same tooth gap, but he had no recollection of *her* being his mother. She didn't look anything like his mum, the one with the dark curly hair, and there wasn't a single photograph of his sister.

In fact when he tried hard to think beyond his life in Portugal he often drew a blank, remembering little. Certainly no memory of being with Gary, his Parr, his whole world.

The campervan was loaded up on the Saturday night ready for their off the following day, but Ethan was subdued and hadn't even packed his toothbrush or spare clothes.

"Parr, I don't want to go without Barns. He doesn't know that we'll be coming back. Look at him, he looks sad. I don't want to leave him on his own: he's used to sleeping on my bed and if I'm not here, where will he sleep? You know that no one here will let him sleep inside their houses, and he'll miss us. Can he come with us, Parr, can he?"

"Mate, he can't! I told you, he doesn't have the necessary paperwork to take him into Spain. I wish he could, believe me,

I'd love us all to go, but it's not possible. Now come on, get in. One of the neighbours will be over every day to feed him and check in on him. Come on."

Ethan stood defiantly next to his dog, deliberating going or staying. "Ok then, I'll stay here with Bernardino and Joao, both of them. You go on your own. You can call both of them every day but I'm not leaving Barns."

"Ethan get in the van!"

"I'm not going."

"Ethan, *GET IN THE VAN!*"

"I'm not going."

And then he ran off down the little tarmac road, right past the social centre, turning round the corner after Bia and Carlos's house, until he found Bernardino's gate open and his great-uncle inside his *Adega* sampling some of his new *aguadente*!

"Ah, *sobrinho,*" he exclaimed, (nephew was good enough for a man as old as Bernardino) you're just in time to help an old man out. Get that funnel and stick it in this bottle while I hold it under the tap."

"Uncle Bernardino, can Barns and I stay with you and Aunt

Maria while Parr goes to Spain for some work?"

"*Falar Portuguese*, boy; *falar Portuguese!*"

"*Desculpe,* Uncle; can me and Barns stay with you until Parr gets back from working in Spain?"

"*Claro!* That's what families are for. We help each other out. Go inside the kitchen, your Aunt Maria has been baking. Go! I'll go and speak with that stubborn father of yours."

"Hey, *amigo*, you think this old man not capable of caring for family. You think Bernardino forget how to look after child? Perhaps because I old man I don't remember what it like for be a kid again, hey? That what you think you English *idiota!*"

Gary was surprised by Bernardino's confrontation, hardly daring to apportion his bravado to his earlier *agua-dente* sampling! The obvious answer to all his questions and accusations was no, but the old man was extremely territorial in whose side he was fighting and Gary was left with no alternative but to go and entrust Ethan into the care of the elders of Bugios.

Chapter 30: River Cottage

Gary's jaw dropped as he cruised up in front of the gates at River Cottage in his campervan, pulling up behind Nuno's old jalopy. *'What an incredible place'* he thought to himself as his eyes skimmed across the river beach with the reflection of the sun sparkling like a huge disco ball, the tall pine tree forest and the mountains. He drank it all in, envying anybody with as much money to be able to afford such a majestic view, one which – in England – would cost millions. His own place in Bugios was gorgeous, but this place was something else. As he climbed out of his van he watched a huge bird circling overhead, some type of eagle, kestrel, buzzard?

"Man," he uttered almost breathlessly, "leave me here for the rest of my life: I think I've died and gone to heaven."

"The very sentiments I uttered when this wonderful man here, showed me the cottage. I knew there and then that I had to have it," Mandy laughed as she walked towards them to open the gates.

"We consider ourselves very lucky indeed, there is nowhere I'd rather be. I'll open the gates so you can drive through and then I'll put the coffee on, unless of course, you'd prefer a beer,

I have some in the fridge?"

"*Cerveja, por favor,*" replied Nuno.

"I'll have the same, a beer, please. I need to savour this moment, this view. Just give me a minute, could you? I'm a bit overwhelmed."

Mandy returned with two bottles of beer and found the two guys sitting cross-legged on her wall looking out onto the river, the sun just beginning to make its descent. She was feeling somewhat smug as she handed the cold bottles over, knowing that what the Englishman was seeing for the first time was the same feeling she experienced every morning as she walked outside with her morning cup of coffee, basking in the selfish euphoria that it was all hers and Kim's.

"My *amigo*, Gary, English same like you. You talk good together and he make strong walls for you."

"Gary, nice to meet you, I'm Mandy. Welcome to River Cottage. My daughter is out at the moment, but you'll meet her later."

"Lady, I've been lured here under false pretences. My *amigo* here assured me this job would be simple, a few days to build some steps and stone walls for you, but now that I'm here I'm pretty certain he underestimated every detail. I hazard a guess those walls and steps could take a lifetime to finish, and that's before I've even seen where you want them."

Mandy liked his sense of humour and found herself laughing at everything he was saying.

All three walked to the top end of the property, beyond the pool, ducking underneath the hanging branches of the mimosa trees.

"It's just here that I want the steps and the wall, I did make an attempt but, as you can see, I failed miserably. I'd like some steps leading up to the top and walls either side. I've got enough rocks to build a path so that I can put some chairs and a table there to create a little 'me' space."

"What's that little building down there?" Gary asked, pointing to an outbuilding below.

"That's the pool room and storage room. The mechanics for the swimming pool, and next to it is a toilet. We did consider extending it and making into a small rental apartment but decided against it. We don't need the money, or the work involved with letting."

Gary nodded in agreement, why indeed would you want the

hassle of strangers encroaching on your paradise if you didn't need to? He was impressed with this Mandy woman; she'd bagged a corker of a property and appeared totally independent. Nuno had told him that she was a single woman living with her teenaged daughter, managing a business between the two of them, but had failed to enlighten him about the woman's obvious attributes. She was beautiful.

She gave him a conducted tour of the inside of the cottage, where each room oozed charm yet simplicity. He was about to open the door leading to her bedroom, but she forestalled him, "Sorry, that's out-of-bounds, haven't made the bed today," she lied, not wanting to witness his pitying reaction when she had to explain away the tens of framed photographs of Nathan on her bedroom walls.

They enjoyed a few more minutes of Mandy's hospitality before Nuno reluctantly bade farewell leaving his two friends to become acquainted and discuss things needing to be done.

"I think I'd like to celebrate this evening with a glass of red wine, or are you a typical Englishman and prefer a beer?"

"I'm not sure I am a typical Englishman or typical any man, actually. I'm just a bloke doing the best he can to provide an alternative life for me and my son. We came over a few years

244

ago, to Portugal, actually. My wife's family is from there, we — rather she — inherited the place. We love it. I'll have a glass of red wine thanks, but what are we celebrating?"

"I am celebrating enjoying the very fact I have someone working on my property that I can actually explain what I want doing without having to resort to using the dictionary to translate everything! It's such a relief to be able to have a conversation with someone without having that cloud of doubt if they understand me. Kim, my daughter, she doesn't have the same problems. She's young, you see. She has Spanish friends and she's picked up the language, but I find it a little more difficult because I don't have the same social opportunities as her."

"My Ethan is exactly the same. He was four years old when we came over to Portugal and he's practically fluent in Portuguese now. He's adored by every single person in our village, and spoilt wicked I tell you because there's not been a child in our village for... I don't recall actually, but probably over thirty years or more. My wife wasn't born in Portugal but her family roots are there, so Ethan belongs to them all. His great-uncle is looking after him while I'm over here; him and his dog."

Mandy was hanging on to Gary's every word. It had been a

long time since she had enjoyed the company and conversation of a good-looking and enigmatic man and one who evidently loved his son! The sun was slowly disappearing over the mountain that graced the river beach, but she hadn't misheard or forgotten the 'wife' comment or the fact that the great-uncle was looking after his son. No mention thereinafter of said wife!

Bryn sat watching Gary digging the structure for the steps as if taking on a supervisory role and running after each large stone that was thrown to one side in readiness to use in the building. It was a comfortable temperature to work in, not cold and not too hot.

"You watch you don't break your teeth, lad, trying to catch these rocks. Don't you have a ball to run after?"

Bryn cocked his head to one side and ran off, returning seconds later with a filthy tennis ball, dropping it at Gary's feet. He picked it up and threw it a long way off, hoping he wouldn't find it and let him carry on doing what he was being paid to do, but Bryn was a clever dog and once again he'd retrieved the object of fun, dropping it on the floor, waiting excitedly to repeat the game.

Kim called out, "Bryn, come away and stop bothering Gary, he's busy and doesn't have time to play 'fetch' with you. Come on, we'll go for a walk to the river later but right now Mum has squeezed some oranges and asked if you would like a glass, Gary?"

"Thank you, Kim, that sounds great. Tell your mum thanks and I'll be down in a couple of minutes."

It was the second day of being in Spain for Gary and he was enjoying his creativity and manual labour of this project. He could picture the end result with Mandy sitting high up on the terrace and surveying the scene of the river below, watching visitors walk their dogs, the fishermen, tourists overnighting in campervans, weekenders gathering round a barbecue or bracing the elements of the deep river, ignoring the 'No Swimming' sign.

He downed tools and went to join the ladies sitting outside on the wall. They were drinking their orange juice whilst discussing some sewing technique Gary had never heard of, the term 'smocking' as alien to his ears as schist was to theirs.

"What do you think, Gary, for the yellow polka dot backless sundress we cut out yesterday? A smocked bodice or a white Peter Pan collar that finishes off at the back of the neck?" Kim and Mandy watched for his response.

Gary burst out laughing as he considered they must be having him on - they apparently weren't and failed to understand the joke. "I think Bryn would be in a better position to give you a more complicit opinion than me, Kim. I'm just a bloke who knows nothing about sewing. I've never even sewn a button on for goodness' sake."

"That's because you have a wife to do that for you. Mum and I have to do everything together, well, practically everything. There are some things that we can't manage but we try our best, don't we Mum? Mum painted the whole of the outside of the cottage because it used to be green and we couldn't stand it, so we painted it all white, she even..."

But Kim stopped talking as she noticed Gary's smile disappear, "Sorry, have I said something wrong?"

"No, no of course not, Kim, you haven't, it's just that... well, no, my wife... yes she did do, she did use to sew buttons on, but my wife died a few years back, so... it's just Ethan and me now."

"Oh crikey, sorry Gary, me and my big mouth. I didn't know."

"Nuno never said anything then, he didn't tell you?"

Mandy and Kim shook their heads, "No, he didn't."

There was an uncomfortable silence for a few seconds while everybody digested Gary's revelation.

"That's why I don't like to leave him, on his own. He's everything to me."

The girls nodded their understanding, they knew only too well that feeling of loss, emptiness, and despair.

"Now, then, I must crack on and get finished. You're not paying me to sit around maudlin over what cannot be changed. I'm a big believer in everything is meant to be, though I've yet to understand the logic. Excuse me ladies, back to the grindstone."

After he'd left and returned to the top terrace, confident he was out of earshot, Mandy said, "Poor fella, I wonder how his wife died? And what a great dad he seems to be, a far cry from your old man, Kim. Can't blame him for moving to Portugal, can you, to be amongst his wife's family?"

Mandy glanced up the pathway to see if he was back at the steps, admiring the man even more with his new proclamation. She knew there wasn't a cat in Hell's chance that Jim would have stepped up to his paternal role if he was in Gary's shoes. Her two would undoubtedly have ended up in foster-care or the like, or even -- knowing the depths of his depravity – sell them to a rich, childless couple. She never understood why she was blinkered by his charms as a young woman, or was it simply a case of turning a blind eye, not interfering with truths you are scared to admit?

What exactly was he doing with his life these days? Was he still a down-and-out tramp like Kim witnessed at the bus station? He must have lost his home, his job, his friends, everything if he was begging on the streets. She was ashamed to admit that she still carried a torch for him even though she knew he didn't deserve it. He had been a despicable husband and father, always seeking that extra thrill never mind who he hurt along the way.

She remembered the first time, and the second and third. The humiliation she endured at the doctors and then again at the hospital. After she reached the point of no return, she vowed she would never allow herself to trust a man, totally, ever again. She wouldn't let her children suffer anymore abandonment or neglect, she was both mother and father to them and felt she had done her very best until the fateful day her youngest had proved her wrong, confirming Jim's accusations of being an incapable mother.

Why? What had made Jim taunt her with such accusations? What mother didn't make mistakes? There was no such thing as the perfect mother, raising children was hard work, dogs were much easier to train.

She wouldn't dare admit to Kim that she was secretly and

selfishly relieved to learn there was no wife waiting for Gary back in Portugal, but she was also aware that he was itching to get back there, to his boy. What other jobs could she find to bring him back once he'd finished the steps and her walls?

Gary stood at the bottom of the formed steps deciding which flat rocks to use for the base. This was the part he enjoyed the most, laying them together making sure the step was even and solid. It was like doing a jigsaw puzzle, slotting pieces together, finding straight edges for the corners.

He was disappointed that Nuno hadn't told the ladies that he was a widower; it would have avoided the unnecessary explanation. For years, he had always tried to steer clear of getting into such discussions and answering personal questions. He liked privacy and anonymity. It was his business, his grief, his conscience.

He liked Mandy; in fact he liked both the girls. He admired them for their tenacity and wherewithal. Kim, he decided, was the perfect daughter and had an incredibly strong relationship with her mother. They looked nothing alike and were not even similar in personalities, but Kim had a maturity Gary hadn't seen in a woman of her tender years.

Mandy, however, had that all essential essence that he felt

beguiled by, and she didn't even know it. He would have liked to get to know her better, but it was impossible. He would never take such a risk. She'd want to get to meet Ethan, perhaps visit them in Portugal, would have seen the television or internet coverage and then everything would be out in the open once the penny dropped. He would certainly go to prison and Ethan would be returned to a family he no longer remembered, in a country where people would hound him forever with questions they'd already decided the wrong answers to.

No. They'd come too far to lose it all over a pretty face. His own heart couldn't afford to be broken again.

Chapter 32: Anniversaries

Mandy's birthday had been and gone. Another of Nathan's birthdays had been and gone, as had another farcical Christmas been endured. Anniversaries and traditions that didn't warrant celebrating, yet had to be, because she still had a daughter to consider.

How time ticked by with no regard to a person's unwillingness to move forward, only a yearning to go back and do everything differently.

She constantly talked to Nathan in the privacy of her solitude, praying he was alive and being cared for. She was confident he wouldn't or couldn't forget her or his sister, or hoped he wouldn't. As a mother she felt she would surely know if he was dead? Wouldn't she feel 'something'?

She hated the missed years of seeing him grow. She despised the normality of everyone and everything around her. She cringed every time she heard a friendly greeting of 'Hi, Mandy, how are you?' Those words 'how are you?' sickened her because she knew she had to answer positively. People didn't want to know, or care, how she really was!

Mac had been her constant knight in shining armour/pain in the backside before she upped sticks and left for Spain. He'd been there to listen to her, yet bring her back to reality with his never-ending barrage of satire quips: "Bint, you're boring me to tears now, other people have lost loved ones too, you know. You're not the only one! But those other people get over it and move on; accept what can't be changed and get a life. Think about your poor daughter and your work colleagues, for crying out loud. All this doom and gloom is getting on everybody's nerves. It's time you bucked up!"

And that was another thing she missed because even though the transition to Spain was just what she and Kim had needed, it was Mac's down-to-earth attitude to everything that she couldn't forget.

She never forgot the conversation with him when she deliberated if she was making the right decision to move away to a foreign country. "But I'm going to struggle with the language, I can't speak any Spanish."

Mac let out an exaggerated sigh, "Woman, you really do make me despair at times. Smiling and laughing, crying and frowning is the same in any language. Body language is universal."

She vaguely remembered one of her birthdays, just weeks prior to Nathan's birth: Jim had been on an overnight the day before, delivering windscreens up in Warrington and she expected him back in time to celebrate. She, him, and their seven-year-old daughter. Kim was excited and had been wearing her party frock all afternoon after she'd got back from school, waiting.

But he didn't come back that night, nor the next. In fact he didn't come back until the night after Nathan's birth. Mandy was broken; she'd taken him back after listening to a million apologies and excuses and hoped this new baby, this new life, would bring him to his senses and they could be a proper family.

And that was the straw that broke the camel's back. Reluctantly, she gave him his final marching orders. Kim had no idea of the depth her previous statement about giving up on him, meant: how could she?

*　*　*　*　*

"Nathan, Sweetie, are you there? Can you feel me? I miss you so much. I hope you're being a good boy because never forget how much I love you and that you will be coming home soon, I promise you.

I've never stopped looking for you and never will do. We have a dog now, Sweetheart. Oh, you will love him! His name is Bryn and he's been waiting so patiently to meet you.

I know you didn't go away without wanting to let us know where you are, and it's not your fault, Nathan, I understand. Your sister and I talk about you every single day and can't wait for us all to be together again. Don't ever forget us, my darling boy. Wait for us."

*   *   *   *   *

"Kim, what did I do wrong to make Mum and Dad send me away? Did I do something bad? I didn't spend the pound, I still have it in my sock. Mr. Parr is kind and Portugal is lovely. You and Mum would like it because it's nice and sunny and warm. I have a dog too, Kim. His name's Barns and I've always wanted to have a dog. I think I remember your friend having a dog, what was his name again?? Bryn? Like my Barns!

I talk to Barns all the time and he's a good dog, he sleeps on my bed. I'm glad I have him. Parr teaches me lots of things because I don't go to school anymore. Did you know we have aunties and uncles here in Portugal, Kim? They all call me Ethan, I think it's because they can't say my real name – 'Nathan.'

Why didn't Mum come and fetch me? Can you tell her I want to come home now? Can you please ask her to come and get me?"

And so the years passed. Too many conversations offered up to the universe that went unheard.

Mandy threw herself into making up their orders spending hours and hours in the sewing room. Anything to take her bizarre thoughts away from the gorgeous Englishman living in Portugal, yet at the same trying to conjure up another project to entice him back again. They could certainly afford to have more work done around their *Quinta*; their business was booming since their notoriety had spread as a result of the magnificent rainbow Greek-goddess dress worn by the beautiful Elizabeth Debicki on the red carpet in London at the Brit Awards.

Kim was beside herself with pride and rightly so. It was one of her very first designs, adapted to suit the request of the acclaimed actress. It was shown everywhere. TV, the Internet, every magazine mentionable and her creations were being highly sought after from celebs to those with royal status.

Mandy had subtly asked Kim to ask Ben and Artur to keep their names and location out of the glare of the press, using only their business name, Manikin, feeling it inappropriate to cash in on the fact that they were the family of 'that missing boy from Leicestershire'.

She knew how the gossip tabloids would portray them and whilst Kim argued that it would be beneficial for the public to recognise them and thus glean more publicity in an attempt to highlight their plight, Mandy didn't share her daughter's views. She also didn't want her ex-husband to cotton on to where they were and how affluent they'd become. She'd seen too many Oprah shows in the past to be under any illusion what Jim would do once he got an inkling of their new prosperity! He'd be selling his stories any which way, slating her and reaping the pounds to pay for his future years of disgusting habits. The press love to dish the dirt and Jim would bask in the glory for as long as the public wanted to listen.

It was too big a risk to take. Jim had even stolen from his own daughter in order to get that ultimate high; there was no limit in his twisted mind. He'd never *ONCE* telephoned her for an update on Nathan! He hadn't even asked Kim about him when he encountered her in Leicester that time, the first time he'd set eyes on her in years.

"I've been considering asking Romero about that plot of land in front of us, see if he'd consider selling it to us," Mandy threw casually to Kim.

"What? But why, Mum? It's full of olive trees and we've

already got five that we never bother harvesting. Why would you want to buy that and create more work? We won't be able to use it and all it means is that we have to let the locals help themselves. It's not as though we even use the oil they give us in return."

Mandy shrugged, "I was just considering that if we did buy that corner, we could extend our driveway and it would be more impressive. Everything we spend on the property will only add value to it."

"But we're not bothered about adding value to it, we're not selling... are we?"

"Kim, the only way I'm leaving here is in a box! I would never consider selling. It has my heart and even if you leave for whatever reason, I still wouldn't. I was just considering adding to our plot and enhancing the entrance, that's all."

Kim studied her mother, with raised eyebrows, "Well, the guys won't be able to do anything for ages. John's told me they're all committed for months now because Christian's bought a mill that he's wanting to renovate and sell on. If you do buy that land you're going to have to wait until at least next year before they can do anything for us. Oh, hang on a minute, you want to get that Gary back over to do it, don't you?"

"Who?" she exclaimed, feigning surprise, "Oh, Gary? I doubt he'd want to come back again. He doesn't like to be away, does he? If you remember, he couldn't wait to finish so he could get back. I wonder if he would though, you know, like a bit of extra work? Should we ask Nuno to give him a call?"

"I suppose it would make sense to ask him that question *before* you commit to the expense of buying a piece of land we don't need," Kim replied sarcastically. "Shall I see if I can find him on Facebook and send him a message rather than asking Nuno to call him? Would hate the poor bloke to feel his nose was being pushed out. What's Gary's last name?"

Mandy thought about it and realised she didn't know, the subject had never arisen to ask about surnames and Facebook friending wasn't something Mandy was passionate about, considering it a distraction; she hadn't invested a great amount of interest having seen the amount of time Kim spent on it and watching people constantly glued to the screens of their phones, laptops, tablets, and what not, the art of good old-fashioned conversation a thing of the past. Everything was sent into the ether using abbreviations and initials she had no chance of deciphering or learning.

She knew they relied on the Internet for Manikin. It paid for their lifestyle, their food, an income to purchase the little corner plot of land she'd set her sights on, but the world functioned sufficiently enough before it was ever heard of and will still keep doing so if it disappeared, she supposed.

Mandy had never been 'into' technology per se; she had an old Nokia mobile phone that still had her English SIM card in, and an iPad she comfortably managed to navigate. She wouldn't even consider downloading a book for example, preferring the feel of a paperback and one of those antiquated things called a bookmark that her daughter ridiculed her over. No, "call me old-fashioned" she'd say, but she'd never been one to follow the masses.

"You could ask him for his number, Kim, then perhaps I could call and run some ideas over with him, and he could tell me if he thinks it's feasible and of course it would totally depend on his willingness to come back and... OR... if he has the time! But then again, he might not have the time or even want to come back to Spain, he didn't like leaving his son, did he? Or should I just forget it and . . ."

"Well, blow me down, you fancy him, don't you?"

"What! Kim, what a stupid thing to say, of course I don't fancy him, I was just considering…"

"Considering a ploy to get him back here, Mother. I've never known you to ramble on so, and blush at the same time. Ha, ha, ha, Mum, don't even try to deny it cos it's written all over your face! Good for you! I was honestly beginning to worry you'd lost the will to ever consider the fact that you might find another man attractive after Dad. Gary's nice, Mum; in fact, he's really nice and if I was an old woman I could quite easily fancy him, too."

Mandy looked aghast at her daughter, reeling over her unfortunate choice of words.

"I am *not* an old woman for starters, and secondly I am not blushing. Thirdly, for your information... and for which is just another reason why I adore you is... that you're absolutely right. I think I do fancy him. Kim, I haven't been able to get the man out of my mind. He is such a nice chap and sooo good-looking isn't he?"

Kim was almost doubled over with laughing, it felt fantastic to hear these words coming from her mother's mouth after all the years of relaying horror stories of her dad and vowing never to get involved with another man.

"Leave it with me, Mum; if I can have a gown I've designed on the red carpets for the elite, I'm pretty sure I'm capable of

266

a bit of matchmaking. We need to get our heads together to ensure we lure him back. You still got those vintage sheets with the embroidered edging? And we need to get you some hair straighteners, you're going a bit frizzy 'round the sides. I'll need to do your toenails too. Can't have you going walking around in flip-flops with those feet. Summer's coming, Mama!"

And then he was there; a feeling of *deja vu* encompassed Mandy as his campervan approached the front gates to River Cottage at precisely the moment of anticipation seeing as though she'd been sitting waiting, watching, timing, the dilemma of greeting him with a chilled fruit juice or practising surprise? She chose the latter option saying she hadn't expected him to arrive until much later, though Gary wasn't convinced of her acting abilities.

They greeted each other with the obligatory cheek-to-cheek kiss and then that awkward hug as to who was to break away first. It was Mandy but it was a reluctant break away as she felt an overwhelming need to last it out, to smell him and feel his muscular body next to hers.

They smiled at each other, both seemingly reluctant to discontinue the initial joyous reunion until a familiar hairy being interrupted their oneness: Bryn! He bounded up to Gary like he was a long lost relative, leaping up then rolling on his back, his pitiful yet gleeful squeals echoing over the river to the fishermen below to wonder what was happening at the little cottage where the two English ladies dwelled.

And it was joyous: Mandy had been planning everything for Gary's anticipated return, dusting places she would never have dreamed of dusting, her kitchen sparkled and smelled of freshly squeezed orange juice, her windows gleamed without a trace of fly blows to be seen.

"Mum, for crying out loud, how many men do you know would notice whether your windows are mucky or not? You seem to be obsessing like Tamsin's mum."

The very words comparing her to 'Tamsin's mum' set her hackles rising and she immediately put her cleaning materials away. Be damned she was going to be compared to the likes of 'Tamsin's mum'!

As par for the course, the evening sun gradually disappeared behind the mountain as the three sat outside discussing what to do with the land in front of the property. (Mandy hadn't dared reveal to Kim that she'd actually gone ahead and put a deposit on it!).

There was a carafe of red wine on the little table, empty beer bottles, the chiminea alight with the branches and cuttings of the olive trees and mimosa although it wasn't a real chiminea in fact, it was the stainless-steel drum of an old washing machine on which more and more fuel was added to the fire in an attempt to prolong the night-time reunion.

Kim excused herself eventually declaring she had to talk John out of getting a tattoo on his butt! He'd been fixating about some Chinese or Japanese monogram which meant goodness knows what! Anyway, it was a plausible enough excuse to give her mother and Gary some space to talk, feeling her presence would only hinder their progress. It was greatly welcomed; they were alone at last, and Mandy knew her daughter would be spending the next however many hours chatting to her friends near and far or creating new designs. More fuel was added to the fire as more alcohol was brought to the table, neither of them wishing for the night to end, to say goodnight, or halt the flow of the easy conversation.

Mandy couldn't remember the last time she had felt so at ease in the company of a man and never once did she feel the necessity to drag up the past about a life in a seemingly altruistic dimension. She didn't want the sympathy vote nor the man's pity: likewise, Gary never veered from the safety of their easy and light-hearted chitchat.

"I think you and I made brave life choices Gary, in cutting ties with the UK and starting all over again in new countries. Once-upon-a-time if ever anyone had told me what my life would have turned out to be and I'd move to another part of the world I'd have thought they were stark raving bonkers, but here we are, me and Kim. And you, what about you? Was it anything you'd considered before?"

Gary was contemplative because the answer was simpler for him. He had a lifeline already in Portugal; as a family they'd been numerous times and the transition wouldn't have been a massive upheaval under normal circumstances: he had a *Quinta* in a village full of elderly people who had little idea about the twenty-first century and all its atrocities. It had been centuries since Portugal had ever participated in any wars and so the locals didn't harbour grudges like the rest of the European countries and in fact welcomed every nationality that settled there. He had never experienced, nor witnessed, any discrimination to foreigners; just the contrary; the cashiers operating the tills in supermarkets, the staff working front-of-house at banks, train and bus stations, medical centres were exceptionally accommodating and friendly.

"I don't like to dwell too much on the past. It's gone and nothing can be done to alter anything. It's like history isn't it, or if you consider the effect of a minute, a second... Have you ever stopped to think about the enormity of a second in time? There... click! One second and it's gone within the snap of a finger. Have you any clue as to how many people and animals on this planet have died in these last few seconds of our conversation? Insects, fish? The list is endless. A split second and everything changes. I live for the moment, Mandy, tomorrow promises nothing, not even our assumption there will even be a tomorrow because for many, there won't be."

"In that case I agree with you that we should live for the moment because our tomorrow may never come, so turn that music up and fill up our glasses. We might both be dead tomorrow."

Gary laughed out loud as he looked at Mandy standing behind the burning washing machine drum, her hand waving the bottle of red wine in the air, her bare shoulders reflecting the transcending moonlight, realising he hadn't felt so relaxed and 'normal', in a long long time. As he stood up to walk towards her to take the bottle so he could pour them both another glass he stubbed his little toe on a boulder that had no right being there causing him to hop and holler expletives a lady's ears should never hear. Now it was Mandy's turn to erupt into fits of laughing as she tried to grab his arm to steady him... and that's when all the laughing suddenly stopped, and they fell into each other's arms.

They lay wrapped around each other, post coital, for the next few minutes, caressing each other and gazing up at the stars whilst listening to the mating call of the frogs down by the river, enjoying the forgotten feeling of intimacy between two lovers. Mandy grabbed her tee shirt to place over her tummy, dreading her stretch marks would be noticed.

"Just listen to those frogs or toads, aren't they noisy?" Mandy giggled.

"They're all waiting for the kiss of a beautiful Princess," he joked back, kissing her briefly on her shoulder. "The river looks beautiful in the moonlight doesn't it, reflecting all those liquorice trees."

Mandy smiled remembering that's what they called them too, then FROZE as everything blurred in an instant. She bolted upright, pulling at her tee shirt in an endeavour to cover her nakedness.

"Liquorice trees. What do you mean 'liquorice trees'?"

"Hah, it's what my Ethan always calls the fir trees, Christmas trees."

"So did *MY Nathan*." She growled.

And just like that, the euphoria disappeared in that split second of time Gary had been talking about. A fraction in time can alter the course of that which had seemed magical, but there was no chance for further explanations as Mandy heard the unforgettable ringtone on her phone, the one she hadn't heard in what seemed forever, the one she'd programmed exclusively to expect news from the one and only Detective Superintendent Sean Doyle!

Naked, she ran to answer the call, her heart palpitating for several reasons, her head spinning from Gary's statement, the possibilities of two boys using the same obscure name for a Christmas tree were too remote to be a coincidence. But it must be simply that, surely? A whopping great coincidence?

"Sean! Oh my God, I can't believe it's you. What? What is it?"

"Mandy, are you sitting down? I'm afraid I have some bad news for you."

By the time Mandy had finished her call, she was wrapped up in her dressing gown, shivering from either shock or what, she didn't know. Her whole body was trembling as she sat alone at the kitchen table trying to digest the news she'd been given and trying to make sense of the last hours she'd spent with Gary!

She needed a stiff drink, a 'proper' drink yet at the same telling herself she ought to keep a clear head to process her thoughts. She wanted to rush straight back outside to confront the man she'd just given herself freely to, to ask about *his* Ethan, but was worried she might possibly be overreacting and if she was, what would he think of her if she were to accuse him of what she dreaded could be the truth? It was beyond real.

And now Doyle had told her that Jim was dead. She had that news to impart to Kim and didn't know how she was going to do it in the state she was in.

Doyle had revealed that her ex-husband had been found by a couple of walkers with their dog under the railroad bridge in Leicester. His partly decomposed body was being held in the morgue where a post-mortem was to be carried out though Doyle had suggested the cause of death was more than likely the result of a drug overdose, due to the paraphernalia surrounding him.

Seconds... that's all it took for everything to change. No chance of turning any clocks back. All those passed seconds made everything history.

Mandy's first priority was to wake Kim and inform her of her father's demise; they needed to be together. Doyle had also informed her that Jim had some personal belongings in his possession and asked if Mandy would be contemplating returning to the UK to make the funeral arrangements and collect the said personal items, but Mandy was steadfast she

276

wouldn't be putting in an appearance and that Doyle could send everything over by courier. At least Kim could have something to remember her dad by.

"Kim! Kim, wake up, I have something important to tell you."

* * * * *

Mandy and Kim sat outside with their morning coffees, in contemplative silence. Gary's campervan was noticeably absent.

"Poor Gary, Mum, he only just got here and now he's gone, I bet he felt he was intruding. Shame, I thought the two of you were getting along nicely? Dad spoilt things again, didn't he?"

Mandy's forehead creased in concentration whilst sipping her coffee, staring across the river, remembering his words as they lay together, *'the river looks beautiful in the moonlight doesn't it, reflecting all those liquorice trees?'*.

"What do you feel about Gary, Kim?"

Kim was taken aback, "I think he's fabulous, Mum! Disregarding his obvious good looks and charisma, I'd say he's the real McCoy. He's fun, he's great to have working on River Cottage, it seems he's a good dad because he's always talking about his boy and I feel sorry for him, it must have been awful to lose his wife that way. Why do you ask that?"

"Well, we have no idea do we, really? We're only judging him on how he portrays himself to us. Perhaps his wife didn't die in a car accident, perhaps he left her, or perhaps he never even had a wife!"

"Blimey, Mum, where has this all stemmed from? I wouldn't for one minute think he'd made it all up, for what reason? Why would anyone lie about having a wife die in a car accident, that's gross, AND he has his son!"

"What if someone lied about those things to cover up a big secret?"

"I think that Dad's death has affected you more than you realise. If you recall, it was Nuno who recommended Gary to us. Nuno knows him *and* his son, has done for years. He wouldn't recommend anyone he didn't trust himself, would he?"

That was true, Mandy acknowledged, but the liquorice tree? It was that simple statement, those two little words that took her breath away: it had been an in-joke for them all because Nathan couldn't pronounce 'Christmas tree' and Mandy had strung several liquorice sweets on the branches amongst the baubles and tinsel.

"Do you know what Gary said last night? He said *'the river looks beautiful in the moonlight doesn't it, reflecting all those liquorice trees'* a split second before Sean phoned."

Kim looked askance at her mother who was staring back appraisingly at Kim to gauge her reaction.

Chapter 35: Thinking Time

Gary arrived back in Bugios in record time, frantic to get away from an excruciatingly awkward situation and thanked God he'd stopped at the Spanish border on his way to River Cottage to refuel, enabling him to get back on a full tank of petrol, cursing his damned stupidity for mentioning Ethan's euphemism of his Christmas tree!

He'd jumped into his van as soon as Mandy went to answer her phone, the past flooding his brain when she emphasised those words *'so did MY Nathan!'*. He cursed Nuno a million times, wishing all kinds of unthinkable atrocities to bestow upon him and yet knowing that it was he himself who was to blame. But he couldn't give in. Perhaps Mandy wouldn't think another thing about it but then he discarded that pathetic thought because his very disappearance was enough to lay guilt at his doorstep.

He was panicking like someone possessed. What were the chances of meeting Ethan's mother? Rather, *Nathan's* mother and sister?

What on Earth were they doing living so close to him? But nothing was certain, he told himself over and over, all he'd said was one little snippet. He'd never shown them any pictures of him, and he had never seen any photographs of Nathan in their house. Mandy hadn't ever disclosed a single hint or clue that she even had a son! He had presumed it was just her and the daughter, exactly as Nuno had described!

Ah, but he did know everything, didn't he? The pieces of the jigsaw puzzle were slotting right into their respective places. He couldn't disguise or hide the truth from himself and as he pulled in front of his little *Quinta* – the traditional Portuguese abode that had been his salvation and safety net – he knew he had major decisions to make, and pronto! If Mandy decided to delve further, to discuss her feelings with the police and he was investigated, his whole world would collapse! She would most certainly tell the police that Nuno knew of his whereabouts and for all he knew they could be on their way now!

Ethan would be snatched amidst the screeching of car tyres, bright lights, a screaming banshee of a mother in hot pursuit, frightening his boy to death, whilst he would be restrained by a mob of angry do-gooders who had no idea… No damned idea…

Barns had heard the familiar slowing of Gary's campervan engine from deep inside the village and came bounding over

282

to greet him as though he'd been gone for years, rolling over and over, jumping up, barking and whining, displaying all the loyalty so few human-beings possess.

Tearfully, Gary knelt to reciprocate his dog's welcome believing himself unworthy of such devotion and then he heard the joyous exclamation of "Parr! You're back early! Oh we have missed you, haven't we Barns? Parr… Guess what we found yesterday? Come and see. Oh Parr, your face is all wet, Barns has made your face all yucky."

Ethan ran inside the house returning seconds later with a huge purplish rock in his arms that he was struggling to carry. It was of varying shades of purple from deep to pale to white, outlined in gold and Gary was dumbstruck as he tried to make sense of what Ethan was saying and what his eyes were seeing! It was undoubtedly the biggest piece of amethyst he'd ever seen and surely that couldn't be real gold! He knew that some of the quartz contained threads of gold, but Ethan's find was beyond imaginable.

"Ethan, oh my God, this is beautiful, where did you find it? Have you shown it to anyone else?" Gary's mind was working overtime.

"*Claro,* Parr. Everyone knows and now they're all digging at the river." Which was just that extra nail in the coffin that Gary did not need.

"Barns found it, he was diving in the water and came up with a small piece at first and then he went down again and didn't come up for ages and Parr, I got really scared because I thought he was going to drown but then he came back up and he had this big rock in his mouth. David Attenborough would be really interested in this wouldn't he? The real one, I mean, not that horrible fake man."

"Indeed, the *real* David Attenborough would very much be interested in this, Ethan. It's fabulous and I'm so proud of you and Barns for finding it, as are the rest of the Bugios folk, I imagine."

"But that wasn't all we found, Parr. Wait here, you won't believe what we found with the metal detector." Ethan ran back inside and came out with his hands full of old misshaped coins.

"Look, Parr, we found some old money. Do you think it's still real?"

Gary was up on his feet, speechless, trying to find the words to describe his shock and excitement. The coins looked medieval, imperfect in their structure, some discoloured whilst others shone brightly. He knew instantly they were made of silver and gold, remembering that gold never tarnishes.

"Ethan! How many more surprises can your old Parr take? This is a magnificent find! It's *real* treasure; I bet this is worth a fortune! Please don't tell me you've told everyone about this, too."

"I'm not that stupid, Parr," he sniggered, I found these yesterday in our meadow. That makes them all ours, doesn't it?"

He didn't know whether to laugh or cry. It was an unbelievable scenario; the amethyst find was one thing, but the coins? Medieval gold coins would undoubtedly contain more pure gold and hence command a hefty return and he should be rejoicing along with Ethan, but... it was Ethan's find and therefore it was up to him what he should do, or rather -- Mandy!

He knew he was finished. His plans of escape were futile as there was no possibility of a quiet retreat since his Ethan and Barns had become an overnight success, putting their small, isolated village on the map for all enthusiastic fortune-hunters.

It was all that Jim Bond's fault from the very beginning, years ago, that piece of shit he loathed and despised from the minute he met him when they were both working for the same company delivering car windscreens, up and down the country, before he packed it all in and returned to teaching.

He loved teaching. It was something he'd wanted to do when he left school, become a teacher like his favourite teacher in high school, Mrs. Atcherly, who taught English and French. Mrs. Atcherly had her favourites, and it was always those who excelled in the subjects she taught, like 'Tally' who couldn't give a damn about anything other than French which warranted him the special love of Mrs. A, who was delighted to learn years later that her loyal pupil had settled down in Corsica to run an organic fruit farm. Her teachings had stood him in good stead after all. The same couldn't be said for insignificant Gary as he didn't reach the dizzy heights of her most adored pupil but that hadn't stopped him from embarking on his own career and spending years at college gaining certificates he would waste before actually being accepted at Hugglescote County primary school, the very school playground he'd noticed young Nathan, the boy who was a dead ringer for his own son.

Sarah had been noncommittal about Gary's 'ramblings', as she dismissed them. Lots of children looked the same, they were kids after all! How was she supposed to know that Gary wasn't the biological father to their baby? She didn't, until she decided to undertake a DNA test after realising the uncanny likeness to the man she had a one-off liaison with. She hadn't the heart to reveal the truth to her husband, knowing her infidelity would destroy him; she decided she bear the weight of her guilt indefinitely.

There had been the company Christmas party, the all-expenses-paid night for every member of staff. The office girls, the factory shop workers, the drivers. Alcohol was as free flowing as phone numbers and email addresses. Mandy hadn't been privy to her husband's company's festivities; according to Jim, partners were excluded, unlike her own fabulous boss. Mac's generous Christmas hospitality knew no boundaries, as was testament to the numerous taxis going backwards and forwards ferrying the young to the city centre nightclubs to continue the frivolities, or the older ones who just wanted to creep inside their duvets with full stomachs hoping not to suffer the inevitable heartburn!

Not that Mandy would have OD'd on alcohol that year as

she was already heavily pregnant! Naively, she believed her husband would have curbed his wayward ways after his diagnosed hepatitis scare and come crawling back to her.

Jim Bond, the Casanova of the entire company and didn't he know it and use it to his advantage as he had always done everywhere he went?

Sarah had looked stunning in her red crochet dress that accentuated her slim figure and long legs and Gary felt proud in introducing her to his colleagues, confident to leave her talking to one and all whilst he circulated amongst his cronies, never envisioning for a moment one of them would move in and work his charms on her.

Naivety and trust. Confidence versus stupidity? Love and blindness. The ingredients all blended together somehow into a pot of cruel reality from which one is expected to climb out from. Does one emerge blasé, having supposedly learned the secrets of life, or are we still as dumb, naive, stupid, blind, unforgiving as ever?

Gary was that Phoenix that arose out of the pits of filth his wife had fallen in because he was the good husband, unlike his vile colleague who spread his wild oats and his diseases at the drop of a hat. He *was* that father for his wife's child because he had no idea that he wasn't!

They say 'the dead cannot speak' but that is not so. The dead speak volumes and louder than the living in some instances - when one stops to listen.

Mandy

It had been a whole twenty-four hours since Mandy received the call from Doyle about Jim, but it wasn't her ex-husband she was mourning, it was Gary. That feeling of being with him had left her wanting him more than she'd ever wanted Jim. Gary hadn't just had sex with her, he'd made *love* to her, and she couldn't stop reliving it and wishing to God she hadn't heard the mention of the liquorice trees or the ringtone on her phone. She wanted to transport herself back to that moment of enjoying being wrapped around his body and feeling safe, loved, wanted.

But he *had* said those words that needed addressing and she felt robbed of the opportunity to delve further. She didn't know his background, where he came from, what he did, only that he moved to Portugal to begin a new life after the alleged death of his wife from the car accident.

What if everything was a complete lie? What - dare she even imagine - his son wasn't Ethan and it was really Nathan? But how could it possibly be that someone – after all these years – wouldn't have recognised him? Nuno would have known, surely. Had Nuno ever seen a photograph of Nathan? If so, then he would be bound to have known...

Should she discuss her worries with Sean or would he assume she was clutching at straws like she felt she was? Perhaps she should dismiss all her wacky ideas and associate her paranoia to the fact that her ex-husband had been rotting away under some railroad bridge full of lethal substances, the man she'd promised in church to love in sickness and in health, blah blah blah.

If everything about Gary was real and true then he deserved a huge apology from her for the accusatory tone she left him with before running off to take a call, which – to Gary's viewpoint – could have been nothing of any great importance. Perhaps he felt hard done to by her actions and wondered who the heck was Nathan? 'My Nathan' she referred to him as. Maybe that's why he left in a hurry, not through guilt but of considering himself insignificant.

She was turning everything over in her mind, going backwards and forwards until realising all the scenarios she was inventing amounted to nothing less than speculation and the only way she would know for certain was to ask someone who would be able to give her some answers. Who *would* be able to give her those answers and what timeframe should she set herself?

The ever mature and sensible of all the Bonds was Kim, who didn't totally share her mother's concern, convinced the most feasible conclusion was that Nathan had been abducted and abused by some disgusting pervert. It was the most logical explanation she could assume. For years, Kim had believed this notion and that his abductor would have murdered him and buried him somewhere too remote to be found. She was well aware that her mother would never acknowledge her point of view, always clinging to a shred of hope that that wasn't the case.

Kim knew only too well how many child abduction cases were never resolved, a small body isn't too difficult to dispose of and Nathan was just another of those sad statistics. Over the years, she had let go of her hope that the police would announce they'd come across his remains somewhere, thus allowing her mother to move on, have some sort of closure after all: but it never happened.

The chances of Nathan being Gary's son, Ethan, were another figment of her mother's over-worked imagination; she despaired. It was blatantly obvious, from her viewpoint, that

Gary was incapable of being anything other than a fabulous person. She could see the joy in his face as he spoke about his boy, his pride and love were evident. There was no possibility of anything further to discuss and she needed to be firm with her mother and tell her she needed to back off or she would soon lose the respect of what very few friends they had.

Of course, that was all well and good in an ideal world, to switch off thoughts and lock them away, concentrate on other important things - like their business! Mandy didn't have that 'on and off' button; that diversion mechanism to alter the course of subject matter; Nathan encompassed her everyday thoughts, had done since the day of his disappearance and would continue to do so until such time that there was confirmation of nothing left to hope for.

DS Doyle had said he would be sending the personal items found on Jim's body, via courier, which was expected to arrive imminently. Neither Mandy nor Kim could hazard a guess as to what that entailed. It surely couldn't be any drugs he would have had on him! Perhaps some money he hadn't managed to squander? That would be most welcome, seeing as though Mandy had no option but to agree to foot the bill for his damned cremation! It seemed such a waste of their hard-earned money to burn him: even in death she was forking out for him.

Next time Nuno came over, she would slip a couple of questions to him, nothing too invasive, just casually ask about the friendship between him and Gary... that kind of thing.

*　*　*　*　*

Kim

Ben and Artur had become Kim's new best friends. They had certainly taken her under their wing, introducing her designs here, there, and everywhere and it seemed she could not fail. One of Ben's most prestigious clients had been booked to attend a wedding in Italy, the millionaire was marrying off his spinster daughter to a very wealthy businessman, and the bride required an exclusive beguiling creation befitting such an occasion, to which Kim was breathless. The only specification was the colour, it HAD to be pale lilac.

The client was in her mid-forties, slim and petite with high cheek bones and long white hair. Ben was going to be styling her hair whilst Po was on-board to perform his magic with her make-up in an effort to make her appear younger than her years. Not that that was necessarily essential because she was, despite her age, a beautiful and elegant woman.

Kim knew that simplicity was more becoming for an older person than frills and flourishes and certainly nothing to detract from the expected extravaganza the bride-to-be would be wearing.

She had received the measurements via Artur's email but knew that, more often than not, they could never be relied on one hundred percent, so in cases of this importance, she made two dresses. One to match the specifications of the client, and a true one which allowed a couple of inches extra on those more important parts of the anatomy like the bust, tummy, and hips! Her foresight was spot on as the second gown fit like a glove and the client was delighted as she smoothed the silk fabric over her form.

It was long without dragging on the floor. She had included three-quarter-length sleeves and a modest neckline to hide all those tell-tale signs of ageing. Plain, simple, but stunning.

Kim, Ben, Po and Artur watched the wedding proceedings in awe from an upstairs balcony of the millionaire's mansion. It was a glorious setting to a magnificent event, each feeling humbled to be participants of the occasion, sipping a glass of champagne they'd been given by one of the beautiful hostesses, knowing they would be leaving shortly to catch their various flights back home which saddened Kim because she adored being in Ben's stimulating company. He could make her laugh with the corniest of quips, and when he, Po, and Artur got under each other's feet their argumentative banter was hilarious. His father was a comedian, he'd told her. She supposed Ben had inherited the same sense of humour and ability to captivate his audience.

He had been the last person she'd opened up to about her brother and he'd listened. She adored him as much as she could ever imagine admiring another person - beside her mother - because of his deep sincerity and normality.

As they each collected their on-board luggage from the boot of the taxi upon arrival at the airport, hugs and kisses exchanged, Ben turned to Kim, "I'm sure you're not going to want to hear this, but I have to tell you anyway. You see, my great-grandmother was what they call 'fey', I only met the old dear a couple of times, but she told me that I inherited her gift which a lot of people say is a load of bunkum but until you've experienced it I guess that's acceptable. She actually told me my future and up to now, she's been dead right. Anyway, I have to pass on messages I receive, and I received a message for you, about your nip, your brother."

Kim looked at him, waiting for him to continue, not understanding where he was going.

"I have a guide," he laughed, "and my guide has told me to tell you that you will be receiving some positive news very soon."

Kim's eyes opened wide.

"Laters, babe, that's all she told me. Call me when you do, she's never wrong."

And with that, he sprinted away to join Po and Artur, who were disappearing in the 'departures' corridor, leaving a bewildered Kim to wonder what he had just left her with.

Bryn's incessant barking alerted Mandy and Kim as they sat at their respective sewing machines on that Tuesday afternoon trying to finish two identical dresses for twin sisters going to their first-ever prom night. Another wealthy American client wanting her seventeen-year-old daughters to stand out in a crowd of 'off-the-peg' prom dresses. To whom they were trying to impress was irrelevant to Manikin's order book! A customer was a customer, and everybody's money was welcome.

"I'll go," said Kim, "probably just the postman. Why can't he just put it in the box and just drive... oh, it's perhaps Dad's stuff!"

She leapt out of her chair, out of the sewing room, running to the top of the driveway as the courier stood waiting. She had to rush back inside to get her passport to prove ownership, sign the magnetic scanner contraption, proffer the Spanish 'thank-you' and hurry back to her mother.

"Mum, it's here, Dad's stuff. Look at the watermark stamp. It's from Sean. Open it quickly."

Mandy scowled at the A4 sized package in Kim's hands cringing to realise that all Jim had to leave in this world was one small A4 envelope. Most parents would have a wealth of possessions to bequeath their offspring, a house, pensions or investments, a lifetime of accumulations. What disappointments lay in store in this pitiful brown paper?

"Kim, not here, not now amongst the debris of cotton and fabric off-cuts. Let's take him outside in the sunshine, let's have a drink – me and you – to savour the moment, come what may. I need to feel a little dignified, it's all we have left."

Kim brought two glasses of red wine to the table outside where her mother sat with the envelope in front of her.

"You open it, Kim," she said as she pushed the envelope towards her taking a drink from the glass, "what treasures has he left for you?"

Kim studied the parchment papers creased to fit inside the packaging, official-looking documents typed in a foreign language. Some photographs were inside too which she immediately recognised as her and Nathan as babies and one other of Nathan that didn't altogether look like Nathan because he had a slight gap between his two front teeth that Kim couldn't recall him ever having. She handed everything over to Mandy once she'd looked through and then opened up the parchment document which appeared to be some sort of property deeds signed over to her father.

"Well, there's no money in the envelope, Kim, but I have to say I'm absolutely gobsmacked that your dad kept these photographs," Mandy said as she studied the dogeared snaps, "I sent him this one of you pair for his birthday. Look how cute you both are. I wonder what he looks like now."

She turned the photograph over to read the words on the back, "Kim aged ten, Nathan three." She looked at the other photograph, "I can't remember this one," and turned it over to see if anything on the back would jog her memory.

"Ethan on his third birthday. Ethan?"

"Mum, let me see!" Kim leaned over to grab the photo from Mandy, staring at the picture in total confusion. "But they look the same!"

"What's that document about, Kim?"

"I'm not sure, Mum. It looks official, like title deeds, look at the bottom page here, there's a solicitors stamp of some sort, dated too... Crikey, two weeks before Nathan disappeared. I can make out some words but it's not in Spanish... and Dad's name is on here. Here's his signature next to another signature, Gary Parr. Who's Gary Parr and how come he sold Dad some property?"

"Gary!" Mandy snarled.

"Oh, for goodness' sake stop obsessing about Gary, Mum. There must be thousands of Garys in the world, it's a common enough name and..."

Mandy stopped Kim short, "And he has a son named Ethan!"

They sat facing each other for a minute, trying to analyse the significance of the coincidences, if that's what it all boiled down to.

"I'm going to call Sean Doyle."

"Mum don't, not yet. Let's not rush into anything we're going to regret. We don't know! I suggest we take this document to a solicitor and ask what this is before we start accusing anyone of anything because if you're wrong, then you will have ruined any chances with Gary that you might have."

"Kim, for crying out loud, what is this photo of Ethan doing in your father's personal belongings? Not just 'any old Ethan' but one who looks the spitting imagine of our Nathan!"

"Do you think Dad had another son, and this is him?"

"Yes, I do, Kim! That's exactly what I think. These two are

almost identical wouldn't you say? Jim must have fathered another child and I don't doubt there are many more!"

"So where would Gary fit into this? He still has his son, even Nuno can confirm that. He showed you a picture of him, remember?"

"He showed me a picture of a little boy whose face I couldn't see because the dog was in the way. I remember thinking something at that time… I dunno… I had this *feeling*."

Kim began to realise how much her mother wanted to believe the son of Gary was Nathan, but it was beyond her comprehension and she was desperately trying to dissuade her from such thoughts as it would devastate her all over again. It didn't make any sense and yet her mother wouldn't let it go.

"Grab your car keys, we'll go and get professional confirmation, find out what this document is before we do anything rash. Who knows, we may have just inherited some foreign mansion for all we know?"

It had cost a whopping two hundred euros for the solicitor to confirm that the document was indeed a property entitlement. Liliana specialised in such matters and, being fluent in both English and French, was happy to enlighten them that the property in Portugal would now legally belong to Kim, once she had completed all the necessary legalities to transfer the title of deeds into her name. She wrote down the address written on the deeds and suggested they drive over to view her inheritance.

It wasn't unusual, Liliana added, because the property hadn't actually been 'sold' to her father, more that the ownership had been 'transferred' -- gratis. Many Portuguese did this as a means to avoid paying extortionate sale taxes, usually ten percent of the sale price, so money often changed hands (in cash) before signatures were committed.

Mandy and Kim left Liliana's office, perplexed. They could only assume that no actual pound notes had been exchanged as Jim had sold anything of value to accommodate his lifestyle, so why would anyone in their right mind *GIVE* him a house in Portugal?

Which brought Mandy back to Gary. He *had* to be the dominating clue; it was far too much of a coincidence to be a coincidence. No matter how much her daughter didn't want to acknowledge her worries, she knew nothing was adding up and she was determined to get to the bottom of it.

That night, Mandy lay in her bed unable to put the light out and sleep. She and Kim had been sitting outside to eat dinner before the sun went down behind the mountain and they needed to grab their dressing gowns as the warmth made a hasty retreat, their conversation topic had remained at a safe level until then.

Her mind was working overtime, again, trying to reason why Jim was the benefactor to a property in Portugal knowing he would never allude to anything that didn't directly benefit him. Why did her ex-husband have a photograph of a child, another boy, who looked like Nathan? Why, unless it was from another mother because that was the most reasonable assumption. She had done the same, sent him pictures of their two children so it made sense to her - as a mother - that she, whoever she was, had done the same.

It was two-thirty in the morning. She reached for her phone on the bedside cabinet and scrolled through her contacts.

'We need to talk...'

Ethan had been so enthusiastic with the treasures he'd found, as had the rest of the villagers who kept telling him how precious he was, as precious as the wonderful pieces of rock being unearthed and brought to the surface.

Gary, however, couldn't share everyone's enthusiasm, he was feeling anxious and lacked the concentration to muster the shared joy, that niggling, sick feeling of utter despair in the pit of his stomach.

He recalled the gleeful smile of Ethan holding his trophy find, picturing the excitement of their adoring neighbours who wouldn't have a clue as to the depths of deceit Gary had gone to secure a better life and future for himself. His selfish self, because he had no right to consider a better or worse life for anyone else.

Would he have done things differently if his Ethan hadn't died in that car accident? Would he have packed everything in and moved to Portugal or would he have stayed put and made do? Of course, the answers to his questions would forever remain unanswered because it was history, he'd done the dirty deeds already.

He remembered the day he discovered Sarah's soul-destroying secret, how could he ever forget an occasion like that? How could he ever forget the moment his life shattered into a million pieces like a broken mirror fallen from the bathroom wall, its slivers of glass reflecting and distorting visions of masculinity, taunting him hideously. It was a piece of paper, that's all it was, a flimsy sheet of paper confirming Jim Bond the paternal father of his son, that little boy who bore absolutely no DNA of his own.

He cried out of self-pity that day. He cried because he knew he could no longer mourn the woman he had married and trusted, he cried because he didn't know how he was going to continue being a grieving husband and father when she had taken away his right. Why had she betrayed him so cruelly?

He hated Jim Bond with a passion, even before he knew what he'd stolen from him. He'd despised his unscrupulous nature, his flippancy and disrespect of anything or anybody. Only women seemed blind to his faults, his very own beloved wife included.

If truth be known, he was never sure why Sarah had actually taken that motorway route that day and it had plagued his mind wondering if she'd been to see *him* again, to show Jim *their* son, perhaps hoping for some reconciliation, reunion?

It had taken a lot of soul-searching for him to pluck up courage to approach the scum bag, after the fatal car accident, to practically blackmail him.

It transpired he'd known all along, but poor old Gary only found out the hard way when going through legal paperwork – marriage certificates, birth certificates, DNA analysis results...

He'd composed a beneficial proposal, he thought, though in hindsight he needn't have been so generous, the man would have taken the King's own shilling! His Portuguese property in exchange for his Nathan.

Doyle had no idea how close he was in his assumption that Jim wasn't involved in his son's disappearance, as it was he who'd accompanied Gary that afternoon to show him where he lived, and what an extra stroke of good luck were they to behold when – like a lamb to the slaughter – there was little Nathan, running an errand to the corner shop!

"Nathan, Mate! It's Dad, fancy bumping into you. Hey, come here, come and meet my friend."

His phone beeped in the pocket of his trousers that lay on the floor next to his bed and he sighed heavily upon seeing the time, two thirty in the morning, and the name displayed on the screen – Mandy.

Gary pulled up in his campervan into the secluded lay-by a couple of kilometres from the Spanish border, turned off his engine and waited until he spotted Mandy's Suzuki Vitara approaching. He was nervous but knew this was going to be the all-out moment of truth, feeling she must suspect everything already and he needed to be able to give his side of the story.

Mandy had told Kim she was meeting again with Liliana, the solicitor they'd approached, to formulate a will. She assured her it was necessary because one never knew what lay in store and she had to be certain there would be no red-tape to deal with should the unforeseeable happen.

She was ready with a bucket load of venom.

She saw him sitting nervously on a bench, his hands knitted tightly in front of him on the table. She got out of her car, handbag over her shoulder, and strode purposely towards him. She sat down on the opposite bench to face him, not wanting to miss any reaction.

"Who are you?" she asked.

"My name is Gary Parr, I'm... "

Mandy cut him off mid-sentence, "I didn't ask your name, I said 'who *ARE* you'?"

He looked up at her stern face, the one that once hung on to and smiled at his every word, the one he wanted to lean over and kiss and convince her that everything he was about to reveal was a lie.

"I'm Ethan's *dad*."

Mandy took out the photograph she'd received in the envelope and placed it in front of him. Gary picked it up.

"Who is this?"

Gary nodded dejectedly, "it's Ethan."

She then placed another photograph of her Nathan in front of him.

"Who is this?"

Gary looked her in the eye, never breaking contact, his heart racing, his heart breaking, the answer choking him, his hands moved to cover his face.

"Ethan's brother."

"You stole my boy."

"My boy was stolen too. First by your husband and then again by fate. I know what it feels like to lose a child too, Mandy."

"And that gave you the right to help yourself to *MINE*?!"

"I was grieving..."

"And you decided to pass your grief to me? You lowlife piece of shit. You're no better than Ethan's father, Nathan's too!"

He glared at her, her words stinging. "Is that right? Is it better to be a father or a dad: what category would you put Jim into because I'm pretty sure I've been a good dad to both."

"You wouldn't understand the word 'good' if it slapped you in the face at a hundred miles an hour, you pathetic bastard! You men... you men... you're all the same. You're heartless, uncaring... Did you know I scrubbed myself until I was raw after you left because I couldn't bear the smell of you on me? I was ashamed of myself for sinking that low, again: at my stupidity to actual *think* that you could be different, but oh no, you're worse, Gary *Parr,* because you *knew,* and you planned it all. You colluded with that pig and *bought* MY son with a measly bit of PAPER! I might have stooped low in my unfortunate choice of men, Mr. Parr, but I have *never* stooped as low as you! The whole bloody WORLD has been on my side, looking for my Nathan! I've never had a whole night's peace, worrying, thinking about him, remembering him. You *knew* where your Ethan was and what had happened to him, you KNEW! You had that knowledge, that peace of mind, and yet you denied the same privilege to me!"

Gary couldn't not face her as he took her every verbal blow, knowing his explanations were futile.

"Mandy, I'm begging you. Please don't break my heart."

"I don't *care* about your hard, insignificant, heart, any more than you cared about breaking mine!"

"Then don't break *his* because you could do, easily. I've loved him, I've loved him the way I loved my own boy, and the way my father loved me, and I'm certain I've loved him more than Jim Bond ever did."

Mandy scoffed, "I bet Ethan's biological father never wanted to know him, did he?" she asked sarcastically, tauntingly, stressing the word 'biological'. "He certainly never bothered about my two, so I'm pretty sure I'm right."

Gary knew a reply wasn't necessary.

"I want to see my son," she demanded, forcefully. "And I don't have another minute to waste. I want to see him... NOW!"

*   *   *   *   *

Kim sat at her laptop, engaging in a video chat with Ben. They were meeting up in London to participate yet again for the annual Fashion Week. It was just the three buddies now, since the lovely Artur had died shortly after their last reunion in Italy for the millionaire's wedding extravaganza. His cause of death was never really acknowledged as AIDS, even though many had gossiped so; cancer was the kinder description.

She had a lot to thank Artur for, he had given her a footing into the world of glamour and notoriety, a far cry from her humble beginnings in the UK.

She was taking John along with her, too, as a special treat and he'd been buzzing with excitement. He'd been out and bought an elegant tuxedo, he'd obtained a passport and he was going to London with his lifelong friend which he'd posted on Facebook a hundred times.

John was the most loyal friend to Kim and likewise she was to him. If life had taught her anything it was the reliance of innocence and the ability to only depend/trust those who reciprocated. She doubted she would ever meet another kindred spirit like John, or Ben, but also knew that it wasn't within the realms of possibility that she never would meet someone she felt able to settle down with, marry, etc.

For now, she lived to enjoy her glorious lifestyle. She was enjoying every single second, minute, and was constantly reminding Ben to convey her thanks to his 'guide,' reassuring him that of course she believed and hoped it was just a matter of time before his 'guide' came up trumps.

'Everything is meant to be' she once reminded her mother and apologised often for her failure to share her mother's beliefs.

*   *   *   *   *

It had taken Mandy a **lot** of resolve to consider Gary's excuses when he had no conception of the years of pain he'd inflicted upon her and Kim, not to mention Nathan, who he'd cunningly suggested calling him Parr, but she also couldn't not acknowledge his undeniable love and devotion.

They had all been victims of one despicable person, Jim Bond, and it was now up to them to ascertain how they were going to go forward. She had every reason to put Gary behind bars which was his just dessert, but was that going to benefit Nathan, and the man he adored as a father? He had already theoretically lost two mothers, a sister, a father and potentially another father – who was the best thing a father could ever be – what psychological affect would that have on him in later years?

Everybody makes choices and decisions, and a split second can change everything, yet sometimes a lifetime can seem nothing more than seconds. Was she about to be the one responsible for her son's further misery? A role reversal scenario. Everything was now in her court, her own happiness and that of another man who had caused her unthinkable grief and sadness.

She had screamed at him, tore at his face, wanting to kill him and cared not a jot about the consequences until she collapsed on his shoulder, sobbing then finding herself thanking him for actually loving her boy instead of what could have been a totally different situation. This man *had* loved him, he'd proved that. What was it he'd said earlier, *'is it better to be a father or a dad: what category would you put Jim into?'*

And then she saw *him*... with that big hairy dog sitting by his side. Her little boy looked practically all grown up - but he was still her little boy - and always had been.

Ethan turned to watch as the campervan pulled into the driveway, surprised to see a lady with dark curly hair sitting in the passenger seat next to his Parr. He had a faint, stirring notion he should know her, confused as to why she was looking over to him, crying yet smiling at the same time.

His Parr remained seated with his arms cradling the steering wheel as he watched the vaguely familiar lady alight the van, hesitantly walking towards to him, extending her arms as if she was going to envelop a fragile piece of glass and he worried, feeling like he should apologise to her because he didn't make it back home from the shop and he still had the pound coin in a little box in his bedroom, but his worries evaporated when the lady with the dark curly hair eventually stood before him.

She was smiling with tears running down her cheeks at the same time nervous to make any physical contact should she scare him away.

A kaleidoscope of memories swam before her eyes. The day she brought him home from the hospital, wincing at every step as the stitches reminded her of the hours of painful labour and childbirth.

His tears and whimpers when he had his first inoculation at Doctor Dunkin's surgery. Kim's ninth birthday party when he sulked because he wanted to be nine, too; disgruntled at not being able to blow the candles out of the Disney-themed birthday cake she'd made.

The day she encountered their bath filled to overflowing with water and the tiny goldfish he'd named – of all things – Rabbit, because he hated the thought of the poor thing swimming round and round in circles in a too-small glass bowl.

She allowed herself rightful gratification for decorating that Christmas tree with liquorice canes because those two little words had just reunited her with her child.

She gradually, and very gently, leaned towards him, allowing herself to hug him, feel him…   and then… *then…* he remembered…

He closed his eyes as his arms automatically reached out to hug her back… "Mum!"

Epilogue

"Bryn, Barns, get here now! Nathan, please help John get the dogs out of the pool, quickly, the taxi's here and I don't want them scaring the driver to death."

Mandy, Gary, and Nathan were about to depart for the UK, for Sean Doyle's funeral. Kim was in New York. It was Fashion Week - again, and she could not let the opportunity slip. Besides, Ben had decided to propose to Po while they were out there and this was an event Kim definitely wanted to be to be a part of. He'd made all the arrangements and it was going to be amazing.

Mandy counted her blessings. She had her son back. She had the man she once loved/hated/and loved again in her life, and her cup runneth over.

Nathan was now Nathan again and he was overjoyed at having his mother back in his life, as well as a loving father. He also had a tidy little nest egg in his own bank account after selling the silver coins and a few of the gold, retaining six as mementos which he kept in a box with a fist-sized piece of the deepest purple amethyst.

Of course, it had taken a long, long time for Mandy to even think of forgiving Gary, considering the unimaginable pain he'd caused her, but her soul-searching brought her – eventually – to acknowledge that by handing him over to the authorities, she would surely lose her son all over again. And Nathan would hate her, his sister, *and* lose Gary. She could not do that to him. Gary had been a wonderful mentor and caring figure in the years and the suffering had to stop somewhere, some day.

John was going to house-sit for the three days they'd all be away, responsible for looking after the two dogs. He felt privileged to be entrusted to look after the place and was looking forward to the party he had planned but not breathed a word about to Mandy or Gary!

Gary loaded their hand-luggage into the boot of the taxi, daunted by the fact that he was actually going to set foot on English soil again, a thing he vowed he'd never do. But Mandy had other ideas. She was determined that this trip was going to be the last time they would ever board a plane again; it was a time for finalising the past, cutting ties and saying goodbyes.

She was going to place flowers on the remembrance wall at the crematorium for Jim; place lilies on Sarah's and Ethan's graves, and she was going to pay her final respects to the wonderful Sean Doyle who had committed years of his life in his endeavour to find her little boy.

Nathan was now fourteen and still retained the passion to emulate his idol, David Attenborough. The selling of the amethyst rocks he'd found only strengthened his ambition to pursue a career in conservation, he had money in his bank account.

The church was full to overflowing with mourners come to pay their final respects to the man who was greatly respected by the Leicestershire community. There was Paula Duff, the young policewoman who accompanied Sean that very first night of Nathan's disappearance. Peggy Simmons was there, too, the news-broadcaster that constantly pestered her for updates.

The entourage left after the coffin was lowered into the freshly dug black hole where DS Doyle was laid to rest and would thereinafter be spoken about in the past tense. Gary held Mandy's hand as they headed off to lay garlands of lilies for Sarah and Ethan.

"Mandy!" She heard a voice cry out, "my husband asked me to keep this safe. I believe he intended you to have this." It was Mrs. Doyle, holding another A4 envelope of mysterious contents.

Mandy looked at the unfamiliar package in her hands and turned to Gary. "What say you, husband? Do we open another Pandora's Box, or let sleeping dogs lie?"

"Chuck it on his grave and let the universe deal with it shall we Nate, Mate? I just want us all to go home please, Louise."

Acknowledgements

Another joyous moment when coming to finalise the end of a book and hoping I have created enough to keep my reader entertained.

When we first arrived in Bugios, in January 2015, we were greeted with the typical Portuguese hospitality of cured meats, home-made breads, eggs, beaming smiles, and words we couldn't understand.

One of the first people I met was Isabel, our caring, enigmatic neighbour who constantly still supplies us with her culinary delights, such as cakes, puddings, eggs, vegetables and salads she grows on her land. A spring-chicken at 66 years old, she never stops working.

Next was Domingo, now in his late 80s, who chatted away to me, smiling, and I had no clue what he was saying. It mattered not. Body language does speak volumes. Domingo – I love you!

Bernadino escorted my (then) 84 year-old parents to his *adega* to sample his divine *vinho tinto* and *agua-dente* and promptly gifted my dad 5 litres of both! Bless you Bernardino, you are the rock of Bugios.

Indeed there were others, now – sadly – no longer here.

My family will never forget the graciousness bestowed upon us when my lovely dad died 13 months after we'd settled here. The compassion of *every* Bugios inhabitant, was unforgettable. Dad loved living here, he told me verbatim, and I laughed every time he mentioned it, like it was the first time.

There is a little community centre here – in our village – where we meet up on Sunday mornings for a coffee, red wine, beer... it doesn't have to be a sunny day to feel the warmth of these wonderful people. You all know who you are...

Now for my British and American supporters. I am always indebted to my lovely ladies, Karen Tyres, Suzanne Bottomley, and Carolyn Irving who have been with me every step of the way, giving me their honest feedback and correcting my many errors. A big thank you once again, to my wonderful mother, Elizabeth Talbott, who reads everything from day one and is confident enough to tell me when and where I need to 'embroider it a bit more', and Carolyn for her final editing perseverance.

Thank you, Mike Hurd, of Lineage Independent Publishing

for all your hard work in getting my words 'out there', for your continued support and friendship.

*   *   *   *   *

Also By Lisa Talbott:

Pen and Inks

Weep and Wail: A Compilation of Poetry and Prose (With Commentary by Michael Paul Hurd)

Spud (everything is meant to be)

A Patch of Yellow

My Name Is Margot

Coming Soon:

The Song of the Execution

The Lady of North Lodge

All of Lisa's books are available in paperback or e-reader versions. Lineage Independent Publishing has ensured that her works will be widely available.